Dex stepped closer, so their bodies were almost touching. 'If I choose to haul you into my arms—' As he spoke, he acted out the words. Iris's heart was hammering wildly against her chest, her mouth was dry, and her mind was blank, save for how he made her feel. 'And kiss you so deeply so we both forget the pain of our pasts, then—'

He didn't get to finish his sentence as Iris urged his head down. Their mouths melded and fused together with such intensity it shocked them both.

The heat, the passion, the power of what they wanted, what they were giving and taking, was filled with pure mutual need. She had never been kissed like this before. His arms were wrapped around her tight, holding her as close to his body as he could get, whilst her hands wound around his neck, her fingers in his hair, as she made sure he didn't, for any reason whatsoever, stop this incredible torture he was subjecting her to.

They were on fire, unable to get enough and desperate for more. Nothing mattered any more. Not the hurtful words they'd said to each other, not the logic dictating they were all wrong for each other, and not the scars on her body which had previously kept them from each other.

This was right. The rest of the world was wrong. Time stood still and raw hunger grew.

Lucy Clark is a husband-and-wife writing team. They enjoy taking holidays with their two children, during which they discuss and develop new ideas for their books using the fantastic Australian scenery. They use their daily walks to talk over characterisation and fine details of the wonderful stories they produce, and are avid movie buffs. They live on the edge of a popular wine district in South Australia, and enjoy spending family time together at weekends.

Recent titles by the same author:

NEW BOSS, NEW-YEAR BRIDE
BRIDE ON THE CHILDREN'S WARD
SURGEON BOSS, BACHELOR DAD
A MOTHER FOR HIS TWINS

A BABY
TO CARE FOR

BY
LUCY CLARK

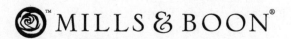
MILLS & BOON®

First published in Great Britain 2009
Large Print edition 2010
Harlequin Mills & Boon Limited,
Eton House, 18-24 Paradise Road,
Richmond, Surrey TW9 1SR

© Anne Clark and Peter Clark 2009

ISBN: 978 0 263 21102 3

Harlequin Mills & Boon policy is to use papers that are
natural, renewable and recyclable products and made
from wood grown in sustainable forests. The logging and
manufacturing process conform to the legal environmental
regulations of the country of origin.

Printed and bound in Great Britain
by CPI Antony Rowe, Chippenham, Wiltshire

A BABY
TO CARE FOR

To my big sister—Kathy.
Your love and support has been inspirational.
Thanks for looking after me. Ps 63:4

CHAPTER ONE

IRIS TENNANT slowed the large four-wheel drive down as she approached the small outback township of Didjabrindagrogalon, known affectionately to its inhabitants as Didja.

She'd been driving for the past three days, across the wide brown land that was her home country of Australia, from Sydney almost to Perth, across the Nullarbor Plains which had seemed endless. Over the past few hours she'd seen the odd tree here and there. Now, though, there seemed to be a plethora of large gum trees on either side of the road, indicating that there was not only life out here but—more importantly—water.

The houses seemed to spring up out of nowhere as though there was a line around the town and you could only build inside it. Iris slowed the car even more as she squinted to see what was up ahead.

'A set of traffic lights?' She shook her head as she brought the car to a stop at the red light. She waited, looking left and right and even checking behind her, but she was presently the only car on the road. She waited even longer, sighing with impatience. She'd had a long three days and whilst she'd enjoyed the driving, she was ready to settle into her new accommodation and sleep for at least fifteen hours straight.

Iris picked up the hard copy of the email her friend Melissa Clarkson had sent. Had she made a wrong turn somewhere? She read the directions again. No. She was right where she was supposed to be—if only the light would change! She sat there for a good five minutes—not another car in sight and the only other moving object on the long, flat road was a tumble weed.

She pressed the loudspeaker button on her mobile phone, pleased she had reception, and dialled Melissa's number. She waited a few seconds yet when the phone was answered, it wasn't a female voice at all.

'Please be advised,' said a deep male voice, 'that the kissing booth is currently closed for afternoon tea. However, if you'd like to come to the Didja oval to collect your kiss in person, the booth will reopen again in ten minutes. Thank you for calling and have a beaut Australia Day!'

'Hello? Hello?' Before Iris could say a word, the call had been disconnected. 'What the…?' She looked around again and saw a blue sign that read OVAL pointing down the street. 'Right. That's it.' She drove the car right through the red-light intersection, down the street towards the Didja oval. 'Kissing booth?' she murmured, her brow creasing into a frown. Whoever had Melissa's phone was obviously at the kissing booth so that was the first place she'd start.

Iris drove along at a snail's pace, heading past the pub, which denied the fact that she had actually entered a ghost town as it was alive with people. Australian flags were everywhere and so were a lot of cars. Utes, minivans, trucks, vehicles of all shapes and sizes—and all covered in layers of reddish-orange dust—were parked around and near the oval, and when Iris finally found a space, she stepped gratefully from the car and stretched out her muscles. She grabbed her phone from the hands-free holder, collected her handbag and locked the car.

As she adjusted her vision to the brighter light outside, Iris searched the wide range of stalls that had been set up on the oval, for the kissing booth. She walked past the hat stall, the knitting stall, the cake stall, the spinning and weaving stall and the 'get your axe sharpened here' stall.

She stopped and shielded her eyes from the glare, looking around. 'Who has a kissing booth?' she muttered, thinking it an outdated and ridiculous custom.

'We do!' a smiling man announced from beside her. Iris turned to look at him and had to stop herself from gaping openly at just how good-looking he was. He was tall—she guessed about six feet five. He had dark unruly brown hair and rich, expressive, brown eyes. There was something oddly familiar about him but she couldn't quite put her finger on it. He was dressed for the occasion in a pair of denim shorts and a cotton shirt with the design of the Australian flag on it. There was a well-worn bush hat on his head and a pair of equally well-worn flip-flops on his feet. He also smelt really good but Iris hadn't come to Didja to ogle the locals. 'It's right this way.'

The tall, dark and handsome stranger tried to link his arm with hers but she managed to evade him. He didn't seem to mind and, after giving her a shrug, they walked together across the dry grass of the oval to the other side. Iris wasn't at all sure what to do. On one level she was indignant that this stranger had tried to touch her but on another level she was too tired to argue and debate. He walked close enough beside her that she could feel the warmth radiating from his body and even being this close to him gave her a funny sense of awareness. She softly shook her head. She must be more exhausted than she'd realised.

'Yep, kissing booth is just over there.' He pointed across the oval as they kept walking. 'I've just had a quick break and now I'm back on duty so you are most definitely in luck.'

Iris wasn't at all sure what he was going on about but if Melissa's phone had been at the kissing booth then there was a good chance she'd find Melissa there, or at least someone who knew where she was.

'In luck?' She frowned at him but he merely grinned and waggled his eyebrows up and down suggestively. He really was very good-looking… But that was beside the point. 'Actually, you might be able to help me. I'm looking for—'

'Oops,' he said as the kissing booth came into view. 'Looks as though the line has grown longer. Sorry. You'll have to get on the end and wait your turn, I'm afraid.' He looked almost disappointed. 'Fair is fair, after all.'

'Dexter!' A woman called, and the man beside Iris waved.

'Coming. I'm coming,' her guide replied. He shoved his hands into his pockets and looked intently into her sunglasses, pleased they weren't the mirrored type as he was able to vaguely see her eyes behind them.

'*You're* Dexter?' Iris looked at him with great intent, recalling Melissa's tales of her brother Dexter and how he was something of a playboy. Never able to settle down with one girl but instead preferring to play a wide and open field. Whilst she could quite easily understand the appeal of the man, gorgeous as he was, he most certainly wasn't her type and she kept her guard in place lest he try and turn that boyish charm she'd heard about in her direction. Add to all of that the fact that he was also one of her new colleagues, given that he worked at the Didja Medical Centre, and that definitely meant any relationship with him would have to remain strictly professional.

'I see my reputation precedes me.' He didn't seem at all perturbed by her knowing who he was. He edged a little closer, his brown eyes intent. 'You *will* come and see me at the kissing booth, won't you?' His tone was quiet and imploring.

'Er…' Iris was lost for words. Did the man hit on every female he met? Or was this simply what they meant about country hospitality? People just jumped right into your life as though they'd known you for ever? Tried to touch you in a too-familiar way? Asked you to visit them at a kissing booth?

'It's all for a good cause,' he went on as though he sensed she needed convincing. 'All proceeds from today's Australia Day fair go to towards getting an ambulance for the town.'

'The town doesn't have an ambulance?' Iris was momentarily stunned.

His smile was wide and utterly gorgeous as he started walking backwards. 'Not yet, but we're extremely optimistic.' With that, he turned and broke into an easy jog. People were milling across the oval and in another instant she'd lost sight of him.

She stood there, trying to get her bearings and wondering whether she was really awake or whether she'd pulled into a parking area and was having a ten-minute nap. A fly landed on her face and she swatted it away. 'Definitely awake,' she whispered. She took a few steps forward, looking for Melissa's brother. 'Good-looking and he knows it,' she murmured, wondering if he would have a horde of women waiting in line for him at that kissing booth. When she eventually found it, she discovered she was right.

Dexter was seated behind a counter, his lips pressed to those of a brunette, who was in front of a redhead, who was in front of a blonde, who was in front of about ten other women of all shapes and sizes. Well, she certainly hoped he was using breath mints. What Iris *hadn't* expected to see was right beside the line of females was a line of very disgruntled males and the lady they were waiting to kiss was none other than her friend Melissa.

'Lis!' Iris dodged the line and walked right up to the front where Melissa was currently lip-locked with a tall, gorgeous man.

'Oi. No sheilas in the blokes' line. Them's the rules,' a man behind her called, but she ignored him. Iris shifted her sunglasses to the top of her head and simply glared at her friend. 'Lis?' Was everyone in this town completely stark raving mad?

Melissa jerked back, tearing her lips from the man she'd been quite amorously kissing. 'Iris! Hi. You made it. Oh, I've been so worried. Why did you insist on driving all that way by yourself? Three days. Three long days in the Australian heat. Anything could have happened.'

'Far more is happening here.' Iris pointed to the man who was still at the front of the line. 'I thought you got engaged?' she whispered.

'I did.' Melissa smiled and ran her fingers through the man's hair. 'Iris, this is my fiancé, Joss Lawson.'

'Iris?' Joss released his fiancée. 'This is Iris? Iris! You're here!' Joss shook her hand warmly, enveloping it with both of his. 'My paediatrician.' He dropped her hand and pulled her forward for a quick hug. Iris looked wide-eyed at Melissa as if to say, What is going on here? Melissa merely shrugged and laughed. 'You're here. Iris, my paediatrician.' Joss let her go and shook her hand again. 'Welcome. Welcome.'

'Don't mind him,' Melissa replied flippantly. 'His first true love is the clinic. I'm coming to terms with it.'

Iris was a little taken aback at Joss's joyous and hearty welcome. 'Er…thanks, I think.' There was a grumble from the men behind them. 'Ah…Joss. You appear to be holding up the line.'

'Oh, I'm not holding it up,' Joss remarked casually as he leaned over the counter and kissed Melissa's lips once more before handing her some more money. 'I *am* the line.' He indicated all the men behind him. 'These fellas just don't know how to take a hint. You're not kissing her,' he told them all, and received a variety of comments as an answer.

'How on earth did you get talked into a kissing booth?' Iris wanted to know.

Melissa jerked her thumb at her brother, who was sitting beside her, kissing the blonde. Gee, he was moving through them quite quickly. 'Dex talked me into it. Said if I wanted to spend time with him, I had to do it at the kissing booth. Well, I can't very well kiss my own brother, now, can I, so that left me with doing a stint on the female side.' Melissa had originally come to Didja to find the brother she'd never known, both of them having been adopted out to different families when they'd been young.

'And it's going to leave me broke,' Joss teased.

'It's for a good cause,' Melissa countered. 'With the funding from the government and today's takings, we should have our very own ambulance in about two months' time! Very exciting.'

As Iris looked at brother and sister side by side, she saw clearly why she'd found Dexter immediately familiar. Dexter and Melissa shared the same colour and shaped eyes, their smiles a little alike as well.

'Anyway, let me introduce you to Dex.'

'We've met,' Dex interjected, having finished with his latest customer. 'Just before. Walking across the oval. A definite connection. It was love at first sight.' His voice was deep and he raised a rakish eyebrow in Iris's direction.

'You're such an over-actor.' Melissa chuckled and turned to Iris. 'He's not even three weeks after surgery and both Joss and I are very concerned about him. I wanted him to take it easy, to stay close, but, no—he's gotta go and volunteer for the kissing booth!'

'Kissing is hardly taxing on the system, Lis.'

Joss chuckled. 'I don't know about that, mate. When I kiss Lis, it's very—'

'All right. Enough of that,' Melissa interjected before Joss said too much.

'Dex!' The woman next in line started complaining that he wasn't giving her his undivided attention, which she'd paid for. Dex, however, was finding it difficult to tear his gaze away from the new lady in town. She had long, strawberry blonde hair, pulled back in one long plait down her back. She was fairly tall, probably around five feet ten, and her build was slight, or at least he thought it was beneath the baggy clothes she wore. However, it was her eyes that held him captivated. The most deep, rich shade of green—like pure emeralds. Her complexion was fair and she had a smattering of freckles over her nose. She also wore no hat and he was instantly concerned that she'd get sunburnt.

He'd heard what Joss had said. This mystery lady was the new paediatrician and Dex couldn't be happier. They'd managed to secure her services for the next six months and even though she appeared over-dressed in her long-sleeved cotton shirt and long cotton trousers, he was most definitely looking forward to working alongside her.

'Dex!'

'Huh?' He snapped out of staring mode and looked back to the line of adoring females waiting for him. 'Right. Must focus.'

Melissa and Joss chuckled.

'Ambulance. Must raise money for an ambulance.' He winked at Iris. 'It's a tough job but someone's got to do it.'

'There's only five more minutes left before my shift is over,' Melissa said to Iris. 'Then we can show you around.'

'Is Dex leaving too?' The woman first in the female line asked.

'I think he's doing an extra—' Melissa started, but Dex quickly cut her off.

'I'm about done.'

'Who's next on the roster to take over?' Melissa asked Joss.

'Me,' came a call from behind Joss, and they all looked around to see a largish man, slightly balding, dressed in a too-tight, too-small football jersey and a pair of equally too-tight football shorts.

'Then quick!' The woman in line grabbed Dex by the lapels of his shirt and pulled him forward, smacking her lips to his.

'Ah…Bluey. You're right on time,' Joss remarked, clapping the man on the back.

'And I'm taking over for Melissa,' a bright bubbly blonde called Bridget said.

'You can start right now if you like,' Joss said as Melissa collected her bag and hat and came around to stand beside him. 'I think the poor men of Didja have been waiting long enough.' Joss kissed his fiancée again before putting his old bush hat on his head. 'Do I have to pay for that one?'

Melissa laughed and took his hand in hers. 'Come on, let's show Iris around. Introduce her to some people.'

At this news, Dex was up and out of his seat so fast he almost knocked the last kissee to the ground. 'Sorry,' he murmured as he came around the booth. His departure was followed by a collective groan of disgust as Bluey stepped up to the plate.

'I can show Iris around,' he said as he caught up to Melissa, Joss and Iris.

Melissa raised an eyebrow. 'It's not like you to walk away from doing your civic duty.' She pointed to the waiting line of females, some of who were deciding to spend their money elsewhere rather than kiss Bluey.

'You feeling all right?' Joss eyed his friend carefully. 'Actually, you're looking a little peaky.'

'Perhaps those females sucked the life right out of him,' Iris commented, and they all chuckled.

Dex merely smiled and said, 'Funny.'

'You don't want to overdo it, Dex,' Melissa added with sisterly concern.

'Oh, my giddy aunt. Will you two old fuddy-duddies stop fussing? I'm fine.' Dex jammed his hat on his head. 'Why don't you go and enjoy yourselves, see some of the other stalls, and I'll show Iris around. You'll be stopping and chatting to people about your up-and-coming wedding and she'll get bored and feel left out. Besides, you'll have plenty of time to really catch up later.'

'But it's no troub—' Melissa began, only to have Joss tug her away.

'Good idea. We'll leave you to it, then.' Joss slipped his arm around her waist. 'I'm looking forward to some real alone time with you,' he said quietly as they headed off.

Iris found herself standing in front of Dex, being subjected to his winning smile. The brown depths of his eyes sparkled and she felt butterflies start to churn in her stomach. The sensation surprised her because she hadn't been instantly attracted to any man since…well, since she'd met her husband.

'So,' he said, and held out his hand. 'We haven't been properly introduced. I'm Dex Crawford. A and E specialist at the clinic, GP extraordinaire and all-round good guy.'

'And Melissa's brother.'

'Well, yeah, and that, too.' He pointed to one of the stalls. 'Want to test your strength? See if you can hit the hammer on the pad and make the bell ring at the top?'

'Not particularly, but thanks for the offer. I'm happy to just wander.' Iris wondered idly if he saw her as his next conquest. The new girl in town. He wasn't her type at all, although she could quite clearly see what the appeal was. He was very hand-some and he was certainly bright and cheerful. Still, he wouldn't get far with her. She had done the relationship thing in the past and it had ended in tragedy. She even had the scars to prove it.

Dex looked at her a little closer. 'Feeling tired after your long drive?' His words were so sincere that they made Iris do a double-take. Had she read him wrong? Did he really care? Was this just a glimpse of his professional bedside manner? Or had she judged him too quickly?

'Er…I'm…I'm fine. Thanks.' She couldn't believe she'd just stuttered. What was it about this man that was making her act so…girly all of a sudden?

'Because I could take you to your apartment now if you like. You could get settled in, change into something lighter.'

Iris visibly bristled. 'I'm fine.' Her words were clipped as she headed off towards the knitting stall without waiting for him.

Dex watched her for a second, astonished at the mask he'd seen her slip into place, effectively shutting him and everyone else out. What had he said that was so wrong? He caught up to her, deciding for now it would be best to let it go. 'Uh… interested in knitting?' he asked.

'Not particularly.' She glanced surreptitiously at him as she picked up a knitted toy and realised she shouldn't be mad at him. He wasn't to know about her skin, he wasn't to know she was scarred both physically and emotionally and, really, he was going out of his way to be friendly and she shouldn't punish him for that. Iris sighed and held out the toy to the lady behind the trading table. 'But I do admire those who are clever enough to make such lovely things. I'd like to buy this one, please.'

Dex watched his new colleague as she conducted the transaction. 'For someone special?' he asked as they walked past the axe-sharpening stall.

Iris nodded. 'Friends of mine have a seven-month-old girl. Anya's her name and she's adorable. They're missionaries and they've just returned overseas.'

'Wow. Whereabouts are they stationed?'

'An island country called Tarparnii. It's in the Pacific, not far from Papua New Guinea.'

'I know where it is. I did a six-month stint there with Pacific Medical Aid about four years ago.'

'Really?' Iris was impressed. Was this another indication of his hidden depths?

'Would I lie to you?' His expression was so deadpan that she couldn't resist laughing.

'I don't know. I've only just met you.'

'And that is why we shall continue to stroll the heat-stricken grass of the Didja oval and remedy that fact.'

'Oh, is that why?'

'Look.' Dex pointed. 'A hat stall. Now, please tell me you have a hat in your car because here in the outback, a hat is essential.'

'No. I'm afraid I don't.'

'Right, then.' Dex picked up a straw hat with bright gerberas on the band and placed it on her head. He studied her for a second, pleased to have the opportunity to really look at her under the guise of checking out the hat. 'Nice, but I think we can do better.' He pointed to the mirror where she could look at her reflection. Iris liked the straw one but agreed with him. 'Next… Hmm… how about this one?'

He placed a bright yellow cotton hat on her head which was in the style of a go-go dancer.

'Definitely not me,' she remarked, her lips twitching at the sight she made.

'Agreed, but you do look very cute. Ah…now, this one is an Aussie classic.' And he dumped a bush hat onto her head which was surrounded by corks that dangled down around her face. 'Keeps the flies away.'

'And gives added protection from kissing booth personnel,' Iris added jiggling her head from side to side as though to prove her point. Their eyes met in the mirror and both of them laughed.

'Would you have worn that if you'd joined the line?'

'Most definitely,' she retorted.

'Thereby making it difficult for me to kiss you.' He was still joking. His eyes were alive with mirth, his lips were pulled into a teasing smile yet Iris was almost positive she detected a hint of underlying seriousness. No. Surely not.

She therefore decided it was best to set the ground rules once and for all, especially given that Dex was her colleague. 'Most definitely,' she repeated.

'What?' He theatrically raised a hand to his heart. 'Iris, you wound me deeply.'

'And I wouldn't even need the hat.' She took off the hat, making sure the dangling corks didn't twist.

'Meaning?'

'Meaning you ain't ever gonna kiss me, buddy. The End.'

Dex's eyes sparked with the challenge. 'Looks as though there's an epilogue to this story,' he murmured as he leaned in closer.

She watched as in slow motion he came closer, closing the distance between them, entering into her personal space which had signs up everywhere reading KEEP OUT. Her mind worked frantically as she came to the realisation that he was planning on kissing her.

Iris was stunned. Utterly and completely stunned at his gall, at his nerve, at his courage. Dex was about to kiss her! Her new colleague was about to press his lips to hers. She couldn't believe it!

Their breath began to mingle, their scents began to intertwine. Her heart rate increased with panic, her eyes widened in tumultuous fear and she did the only thing she could think of to stop him.

Iris raised her hand and slapped Dex soundly across the cheek.

CHAPTER TWO

THE reverberating sound surprised them both.

Several people, including a lot of women who were milling around them, all gasped in shock at what had just happened. Someone had slapped Dexter Crawford!

Iris instantly covered her mouth with her hand as mortification ripped through her. 'Oh, my gosh. Dex. I'm sorry.'

Dex stepped back, putting distance between them, and rubbed his cheek. 'Nice shot.'

'It was reflex. A reaction. I just don't like being touched. Especially by strangers.' She reached out to touch his cheek but thought better of it. 'You have my handprint on your cheek.'

'Don't mind him, deary,' the woman manning the hat stall said. 'He's had worse than that before, ain't ya, Doc?'

'You are correct, Minerva.' Dex nodded and smiled at Iris. 'It was my fault. I shouldn't have let my impulses get the better of me. Especially when I'm trying so hard to make a good impression on my new colleague.'

Minerva chuckled. 'Looks more like she's left an impression on you, mate.' And she pointed to his still-red cheek.

'True.' Dex looked at the hats, needing to change the subject and move things along. 'How about this one?' He handed her a navy-blue cloth hat which would well and truly provide enough covering for her delicate, fair skin. It had white piping around the edge which folded up into a brim. Iris put the hat on, liking the snug fit and knowing it wouldn't blow off on windy days. She looked at herself in the mirror and met Dex's reflection. His eyes were intense, his voice soft so that only she could hear it.

'I like that one the best. It really suits you. Frames your beautiful face to perfection.'

She shouldn't allow herself to be swayed by his words. No doubt he spoke to every woman in town this way, so intensely, so personally. He had the ability to make her feel as though nothing else mattered except her. That she alone was worthy of his one hundred per cent undivided attention and part of her really liked that feeling.

The other part—the sensible part—told her not to believe a word he was saying. Trusting Dex Crawford in a personal capacity would only lead to trouble, of that she was certain, and so she schooled her thoughts and tore her gaze away from his and looked at Minerva.

'I'll get this one, thank you.'

'Oh, please. Allow me.' Dex was quick to pull out his wallet.

'It's fine. I've got it.'

'But it could be a welcome gift. Or even an apology for my impetuous behaviour.'

'All is forgiven,' she said firmly, handing over the money. 'I'm a big girl, Dex, and I can look after myself. I've been doing it for years now without your assistance.'

Dex knew women and he knew when to back down. 'Fair enough.' He put his wallet away and waited for her to complete the transaction.

Minerva cut the tag off the hat and Iris continued to wear it, liking the fact that it gave her even more of a shield against the charming Dexter Crawford. He really did have charm and charisma in abundance and she could quite see why there had been so many women lining up to kiss him.

'So, where to next? Need to get your axe sharpened? Or perhaps you're hungry? There's a great stall over there.' He pointed across the oval to where a long line of people were waiting to be served whilst others sat on the chairs and tables provided to eat their fare. 'Stiggie's. Stig owns a restaurant in town—well, really it's the only proper restaurant in town so I guess it's just as well that he serves the most mouth-watering food around.'

'Stiggie's?' They started to walk towards the food stall, which was situated in the main clubhouse building. Iris guessed it was far easier to serve warm food from a place where electricity was readily available.

'Yeah. Stig is a small Italian bloke who's been in Didja a lot longer than I have. Goodness knows what made him come out from Italy and settle in the middle of nowhere, but he did and our gastronomic juices have been for ever grateful.'

Iris smiled at his words. 'Well, so long as the gastronomic juices are grateful, what else matters?'

Dex grinned at her. 'My sentiments exactly, Dr…' He paused. 'I'm sorry. I've forgotten your surname.'

'And yet you've tried to kiss me. Do you often go around kissing girls whose names you don't even know?'

Dex exhaled harshly at her words and frowned

a little. 'Ooh. If I answer that question, I'm afraid I might incriminate myself and sink even lower in your estimation.'

'Oh, you can answer. You're already at the bottom so there's nowhere else for you to sink,' she retorted calmly.

'Ouch.' Dex grinned at her. 'You really don't believe in pulling your punches. I like that about you. Beautiful, smart and honest.'

'A lethal combination?' He thought she was beautiful? Iris brushed the thought away, reminding herself he knew how to flatter and flirt to perfection. She'd do best not to take anything he said seriously. Still…it was kind of nice being told she was beautiful.

'Most definitely.' They walked a little further. 'And you still haven't told me your surname.'

'Do you often forget colleague's surnames?'

'I do when I get lost in vivid eyes the colour of emeralds.'

Iris chuckled at his overblown compliment. 'Real smooth.'

Dex grinned. 'Come on, Iris. It's not as though it's a great secret. Besides, we're not only going to be colleagues, we're neighbours as well.'

'What?' Iris was surprised at his words.

'Melissa didn't tell you about the accommodation?'

'She said there was a furnished apartment provided.'

'There is. There's an apartment complex of four units at the rear of the clinic. Nice and close to work and nice and close to your colleagues.'

'Melissa and Joss live there too?'

'They do, although they're currently looking for a house of their own in town. They may end up building but that's yet to be seen. At any rate, after their wedding, it will just be you and I in the complex.' He spread his hands wide as though there was nothing he could do about it. 'Neighbours. That's us.'

'Tennant.'

'Well, yes, I guess you could say we'll be tenants by living next door to each other. That still means we're neighbours.'

'No. I mean my surname is Tennant.' She spelt it out for him.

'Oh. That's right.' He mulled her name over for a second. 'Dr Tennant. Dr Iris Tennant.'

'That's me.'

'I do remember now. Thank you for jogging my memory. So tell me, Dr Iris Tennant, were you teased as a child with a surname like that? Did people think you'd come to their place to stay? To be their tenant? Or weren't they smart enough to figure it out?'

Iris shook her head. 'I wasn't teased at all.' She stopped walking for a second and met Dex's intense gaze. Raising one eyebrow, she delivered the line she hoped would stop his constant attempts to flirt with her—at least for the time being until he found out the truth. 'You see, Tennant is my married name.' With that, she walked off, leaving him gaping open-mouthed after her.

Married! She was *married!*

She didn't wear a wedding ring. In fact, she didn't wear any jewellery at all except for a pair of gold earrings. Then again, he knew a lot of doctors who didn't wear wedding rings but most of them were male. He shrugged, guessing it wasn't only men who didn't wear wedding bands. And where was her husband? Had she come on ahead to get settled in? Would he be here in a week or two? Dex realised he would have to start paying better attention in the clinic business meetings Joss made them hold on a regular basis.

He watched Iris, consigning her to the 'look but don't touch' category in his mind. Married? Dex shook his head as though trying to clear the thought from it. Checking for wedding bands was usually one of the first things he did when he spied a pretty woman—he'd check her hands for signs of commitment rings. If there were none, he felt free to at least flirt a little. He would never call himself a womanizer. Rather, Dex thought of himself more as a determined flirt but with a heart of gold. He would never intentionally set out to hurt anyone and the women he socialised with all knew the score. He was friends with everyone and had a commitment to no-one. He was all about having fun and it was top of his priority list.

Back in his early university days, he'd thought he'd found the woman of his dreams. Catherine. Gorgeous, untouchable Catherine. She'd been gorgeous and he'd been way too attentive. They'd dated for almost a year before she'd calmly told him it was over. He'd been smothering her with so much affection, she couldn't breathe. She continued shoving metaphoric knives into his heart by telling him she wanted nothing more to do with him and that she'd actually started seeing another man who was already a qualified doctor, not one still in training.

To say this had come as a shock to Dex was an

understatement. He'd always classed himself as a true romantic and had plied Catherine with candle-lit dinners, flowers, her favourite perfume and many other gifts. Yes, he'd been jealous if she'd even spoken to another man but he'd thought he'd handled it well enough. He hadn't ranted or raved. He hadn't even questioned her about it but, in all fairness to her, he'd wanted to make sure that every spare moment she'd had she'd spent with him. He hadn't been able to understand why she wouldn't. Why she hadn't wanted to be with him as much as he'd wanted to be with her. He'd loved her. He'd *really* loved her.

And he'd smothered her right out of his life.

He closed his eyes for a brief second and shook his head. He hated thinking about his past shame, of what he'd been back then. The break-up had affected him greatly, so much so that his grades had started to slip during the next few years of medical school. Then he'd met Joss. Joss had agreed to tutor him and a strong and abiding friendship had developed. And he'd vowed that never again would he be suckered in by a woman. He would keep his heart aloof, under control, and just be friendly to everyone!

Dex opened his eyes and watched Iris walking

ahead of him. Here was another woman who seemed determined to snub him, to put him in his place. She was married. He had to remember that. Still, his new colleague was so devastatingly gorgeous he was having a difficult time keeping his thoughts in check. He was usually attracted to blondes but Iris Tennant had proved to be a most intriguing strawberry blonde with eyes so richly deep he felt as though he was swimming in liquid jade. Mesmerising. She was utterly mesmerising and he hadn't been so mesmerised by a woman since Catherine.

He would not pursue her, not in a romantic vein. He couldn't. She was married. However, he did intend to be personable, to show her around and to introduce her to the delights of Didja. Her contract was only for six months yet he knew Joss was hoping that once Iris could see how wonderful life was here, she would choose to stay longer.

Dex watched as she perused the chalk-board menu Stig had written up that morning. She had a lovely figure, well, what he could see of it as her cotton shirt was hanging loosely over her trousers. She was tall, too, which he liked. Taller than the average woman but, then, he was taller than the average male and therefore Iris fitted by his side perfectly. Indeed, when he'd swooped down, intending to kiss her, he hadn't needed to bend too far.

And then she'd slapped him. His lips curved into a smile at the memory. Beauty, intelligence and a fiery temper to boot. He liked a woman with spirit, one who wouldn't fawn at his feet. Too bad she'd already been snapped up by another man. 'Look but don't touch,' he warned himself softly as he walked over to where she stood. Colleagues. Friends. Nothing more.

She didn't turn around to look at him but merely asked, 'What's a schnitzel stick?'

'Ah, now, that's one of Stig's own delicacies. It's cooked schnitzel meat on a skewer.' He shrugged a shoulder. 'Makes it easier to eat at events such as these.'

'You've had one?' She turned to look at him and was surprised to find him standing closer than she'd realised. She had hoped that mentioning that Tennant was her married name might make Dexter back off slightly. Apparently she'd under-estimated him for he seemed just as interested as ever in escorting her around the fair.

'Of course. I've tried everything Stig makes.'

Before she could say another word, he'd walked

into the building, opened the door and stepped behind the counter into the small kitchen. Iris watched through the large serving window as Dex simply helped himself to two schnitzels on sticks.

'Doc Dex. You know you're not allowed back here,' said a man with a relaxed Italian accent. Iris presumed this was the chef himself—Stig. There were three other people in the kitchen, all cooking and preparing food, yet Dex had simply jumped the line, not caring what anyone said or did.

'I know,' Dex remarked as he paid for the food. 'And I'm sorry but I'm desperately trying to impress our brand-new paediatrician, who'll be working at the clinic for the next six months.' He spoke loud enough for quite a few people to hear and soon Iris found herself subjected to quite a lot of interested stares.

'Another sheila doc!' Stig beamed brightly and started clapping his hands. 'Welcome. Welcome to Didja,' he hollered, and Iris stretched a polite smile across her lips. 'Take the schnitzel,' Stig was urging Dex as he left. 'You let me know what you think of my food,' Stig called to her and Iris nodded. 'You come by my restaurant. I'll give you a good meal.'

'I'll make sure she does,' Dex remarked with a

wink. 'Book us a table for Saturday night,' he called back as he walked over to where Iris was standing.

'Aw, Doc Dex. You are bad.' Stig laughed and went back to serving customers.

'Here.' Dex held out the schnitzel stick and a napkin. 'No more need for forks.' He took a bite of his. 'Mmm. So good,' he murmured. 'Try it.'

Iris realised there were a few interested people still watching her and though she badly wanted to offer Dex payment for the food, because she was a woman who didn't rely on anyone, she decided to forego that for the moment and instead sampled the food.

Dex was watching her intently and was pleased when her eyebrows lifted in happy surprise. 'Mmm. Delicious.' He turned and gave Stig a thumbs-up. A few people clapped and then went back to what they were doing. Iris took another bite.

'Really delicious,' she said after she'd swallowed her mouthful. 'He should market these. They'd sell so well all around the country.'

Dex nodded. 'Agreed, but, you see, our Stig isn't after worldwide fame and fortune. For some strange reason, he's more than content to live here and provide the township of Didja and surrounding communities with amazing food.' He grinned at Iris. 'And all I can say to that is amen!'

She laughed, annoyed with herself for liking Dex so much. He was a determined flirt who no doubt had a harem of women falling at his feet on a regular basis. He was extremely good-looking—and knew it. He seemed to relate easily to everyone he met, whether male or female, old or young and everyone, in turn, seemed to love him back.

Well, she hadn't come to Didja to love him. In fact, that wasn't even on her list of things to achieve in the next six months. Dex would simply be another colleague to her. Nothing more. She was here to provide a medical service to an outback community. Not only would the appointment look good on her résumé but it gave her the opportunity to escape from her life and that had been the biggest draw when Melissa had first suggested she come to Didja.

She had a job to do and she'd do it. She had goals to achieve and she'd achieve them. Being head of paediatrics at a busy teaching hospital in Melbourne was high on her list and coming to Didja would most definitely help. Then she would move from Sydney to Victoria to the Royal Children's hospital and away from her past. She'd already broken the mould by coming here, by venturing to do something different, and she hoped it would help her to put her previous life behind her once and for all.

They both finished eating and Dex looked at her. 'Want another one?'

'Perhaps later, although they were extremely good.'

'Told you so.'

'Yes you did. You're a man who knows his schnitzel sticks.'

'Thank you, Iris. Such a compliment from a woman of your calibre is something I shall treasure for ever.'

She smiled and shook her head. 'Melissa was right. You are such an over-actor.'

Dex leaned a little closer and said in a stage whisper, 'It's already on my résumé.'

His hypnotic, earthy scent wove around her and she tried not to like it. There was heat radiating from his body as his lips twitched into a smile. Iris took a step backwards, not liking the mildly intimate atmosphere he'd created. 'Glad to hear it.' She tried to keep her tone brisk and impersonal but wasn't sure she'd succeeded.

'So…' He clapped his hands together. 'Where

to next? What would you like to see? More stalls? Or perhaps the pub? It is the main hub of the town.'

Iris thought for a moment, unsure what to do. She decided it was best if there were people around them—lots of people—wherever they went. When she'd driven by the pub earlier, she had noticed it was relatively full. Yet the fair atmosphere would provide less time for personal chit-chat as there was so much to comment on.

'Perhaps another stall,' she remarked. 'After all, I hear that the district does need an ambulance. Best get to spending our money.'

'Yes, we should.' And he stepped forwards to link his arm with hers as he'd tried to do when she'd first arrived.

'We don't need to do that,' she said, stepping back from him again.

Dex held up his hands in surrender. There was definitely a big NO TOUCHING sign above her head and he could respect that. 'Fair enough. Was just trying to be neighbourly.' He indicated to the stalls with an open hand. 'Would you like to go to the cake stall? The second-hand clothing stall? The jewellery stall? The kissing booth?' He raised an eyebrow suggestively. 'I could take another turn if you'd prefer to spend your money wisely?'

Iris shrugged and started walking off. 'Oh, I don't know. That Bluey chap looked OK.'

Dex nearly choked on his tongue and she couldn't help but laugh. 'What would your husband say about that, I wonder?' he asked, unashamedly fishing.

Before Iris had time to respond, a woman started shrieking at the top of her lungs.

'Help! Help! He's choking. Watson. Stop it. Help! Somebody!'

Dex and Iris wasted no time, both doing an about-face as they headed in the direction of the cry for help. It was coming from the area where people could sit and relax whilst they ate.

'He's choking!' The woman continued to yell.

'Hit him on the back,' someone suggested.

'No, put your arms around his waist and pull,' someone else suggested.

'Doc Dex? Doc Dex!' Stig was calling for him.

'I'm here,' Dex called over the hullabaloo. At the back of the area Stig had set up with tables and chairs for his patrons, a young boy, Watson, who was seven years old, was frantically trying to suck air into his lungs.

'Stand back,' Dex ordered. 'Give him some room.' He lifted the boy to his feet and wrapped his arms around the upper part of the abdomen. Clasping his hands into a fist, he suddenly and firmly forced them upwards into the gap between the lower ribs, hoping the compression of air in the chest would expel the bolus of food.

It didn't. Watson continued to gasp for air, his mother screaming hysterically. Iris came up behind Dex.

'Bend him slightly forward,' she instructed, and Dex obeyed. He kept Watson's head as low as possible whilst Iris struck the seven-year-old firmly between the shoulder blades with the heel of her hand.

Nothing!

A crowd was beginning to gather, everyone hovering with mounting anxiety. Iris thought quickly and looked at Stig, who was dithering nearby.

'Is there a vacuum cleaner? Find a vacuum cleaner. Plug it in, bring it here.' She knew it was a risky solution but if she didn't try something soon, Watson would choke to death.

'The new doc's barmy,' a bloke called.

'Just do it,' Iris insisted, her tone brooking no argument. Stig rushed off to do her bidding. Dex was soothing Watson trying to get the child to relax his body in the hope that a smidgen of air could continue to make its way through until they'd dislodged the obstruction.

While they waited, Dex held the boy in position whilst Iris struck him firmly between the shoulder blades again. Still nothing.

'Try and relax your muscles,' Dex told Watson. 'It's all right. We're here. We're going to help you.'

'Has someone called for a—?' Iris stopped, only then remembering that the town didn't have an ambulance. Not yet. 'A bucket. I'm going to need a bucket.'

'You all right, Doc?' A woman asked.

'The bucket's not for me,' she said with a touch of impatience. What was taking them so long with the vacuum cleaner? Why did everything seem to be happening in slow motion?

'Tip his head back and try and blow some air past the obstruction,' she suggested to Dex, but even as the words left her mouth Dex was already shifting Watson around to do just that.

'Here it is,' a person called, and Iris turned to see Stig running towards them with an old vacuum cleaner.

'Plug it in,' she urged as she pulled the head off the vacuum, getting the nozzle ready.

'All right.' Stig yelled across the room. 'It's in.'

Iris tested the suction and found it wasn't too strong for picking up dirt but it was better for what she was about to do. 'Suction is ready. Sit him upright,' she instructed, and Dex complied, holding Watson's jaw down and open, whispering quietly and reassuringly in the boy's ear. Iris placed the vacuum cleaner pipe into Watson's mouth, ensuring the tongue was depressed. The poor child started gagging as the suction began but Dex held him firm, as well as delivering a few more blows between his shoulder blades.

Within seconds, the blockage was cleared and Iris carefully removed the pipe. A collective sigh of relief rippled through the crowd and Watson collapsed against Dex, who held the boy, soothing him.

'Bucket.' Iris held out her hand, her eyes still watching their patient. She accepted the bucket and placed it in front of Watson who, seconds later, started to retch. She watched as Dex continued to hold the boy, talking calmly. The poor boy was still as white as a sheet but was now completely out of danger. Dex was certainly very good with children and obviously had a calming bedside manner. She was impressed.

Iris looked over to where Watson's mother was

crumpled in a heap on the floor, friends crouched down beside her, rubbing her back and supporting her as she cried. And quite right, too. Seeing your son choke was a highly traumatic event. After years of treating children, Iris knew it was often the parents who reacted more than the child.

When Watson was finished, Iris handed the bucket to someone and took the boy's pulse. It was still elevated but slowly returning to normal. 'How are you feeling?' she asked him.

'Tired.'

Both Dex and Iris smiled at the answer. 'That's to be expected. Your throat's going to be sore for the next few days.'

'And that means,' Dex continued, Watson still in his arms, leaning heavily against him, 'no talking loudly, no singing, no yelling at your sisters.'

'Not fair,' Watson whispered, but nodded.

'I think we'll have you stay at the hospital tonight,' Iris said. 'Just so we can monitor you.' Watson's eyes grew wider at this information.

'It's just overnight,' Dex reassured the young boy. 'And you'll have Bub looking after you, and you like Bub. And you'll have to eat soft, mushy foods.'

'Like puréed spinach?' Watson whispered, and wrinkled his nose. Iris found it difficult not to laugh.

'I think we can do better than that.' Dex chuckled and she tried not to let the sound wash over her. The man really did have the sexiest laugh she'd ever heard. So smooth, so rich and so genuine. 'Like… Oh, I don't know. What do you think, Dr Iris? Ice cream?'

She snapped her attention back to what was happening, rather than being concerned about Dexter Crawford's husky laugh. 'Hmm.' She pretended to think for a second. 'Ice cream, eh? That might do.' She looked at Watson and snapped her fingers. 'Oh, I know. What about jelly?'

'And custard.' Dex nodded and licked his lips. 'I think I'm going to enjoy visiting you in hospital. Maybe you'll share?'

Watson grinned and shook his head. Iris was pleased there was colour coming back into the boy's cheeks. He'd had a terrible scare but he'd do just fine.

'Well…OK, then. I guess that's fair,' Dex remarked. 'But you do know there's something extra-special about you now.'

'What?' Watson whispered.

'You're Dr Iris's first patient in Didja.' He nodded. 'And what a fine initiation it was for her.' He looked at the crowd around them. 'What d'ya say, mates? How about a big round of applause for our new resident paediatrician—Doc Iris.'

And indeed a round of applause was exactly what she received. Iris felt highly self-conscious as she stood and smiled, politely accepting the thanks from the people of this strange but loving outback town.

She glanced down at Dex who winked at her, then treated her to one of those butterfly-inducing smiles. His tone was warm and inviting as he said more quietly, 'Welcome to Didja, Iris.'

CHAPTER THREE

THE clinic, which had a little ten-bed hospital at the rear of the premises, wasn't what Iris had been expecting.

They'd bundled Watson into the rear of her four-wheel drive, Watson's mother beside him and Dex sitting in the front passenger seat, exuding way too much heat and male phero-mones for Iris's liking. Thankfully, the drive had been relatively short and Dex had directed her to park the car around the rear of the building.

'That's where we live.' He pointed to a set of four ground-level apartments, which were separ-ated from the clinic by the small and private car park they were in. Even Dex's words—'That's where *we* live'—made her want to blush, made her want to correct him and point out that they weren't, in fact, *living* together but rather sharing an apartment block. Then again, she knew she'd only be arguing semantics and it would only show

Dex how much his words had affected her. Besides, they had a patient to deal with.

As they headed inside, Dex carrying young Watson whilst the boy's mother trailed behind, Iris marvelled at the difference between outback medicine and that of its counterpart in the city. A wheelchair would have been provided for Watson back in Sydney to transport him from the vehicle—which would have been an ambulance—into the sanctuary of the hospital building. There would have been paperwork to be filled out and red tape to be processed. Insurance. Public liability. Doing everything by the book. Instead, she'd driven the patient to the hospital in her own vehicle and Dex had carried the patient inside, talking animatedly to him as they went.

He was very good, very natural with the boy, and she wondered if he was like this with all of his patients. She knew he had the charm and charisma to seriously affect the female population but it appeared Dex could charm anyone, regardless of age, race or sex. He was obviously well liked and respected within the community and for that reason Iris decided to try and control her need to make snap judgements, to pigeonhole people and put them in a box marked 'X' so she could deal with them in a less personal way—and she would start with Dex.

She watched as he placed Watson on a bed and made sure both mother and son were comfortable before performing observations on their patient. Again, this was something a nurse would usually have done but it appeared out here in the outback it was all hands on deck. Hierarchy and rank appeared to have little or no consequence at all. At least, this was what she thought until she met Bub.

'Dexter. I see you've brought me another patient,' Bub said as she came over and embraced Watson's mother. Iris guessed Bub to be a woman in her mid to late fifties. She had short grey hair and a weathered smile. Her eyes were bright with teasing as she shooed Dex away, taking the stethoscope from him and making him stand at the end of the bed.

'Out of the way. It's my job so let me do it.'

'I was just trying to help.' Dex sounded a lot like a scolded little boy. He turned and looked at Iris, winking at her which let her know that Bub really wasn't as cross with him as she'd sounded. 'Watson decided to breathe and eat at the same time,' Dex said in an attempt to give some sort of handover. 'Which resulted in—'

'I know what happened. I've had at least twelve calls from various people letting me know what to expect.' Bub turned and looked directly at Iris. 'Honestly, darl, in this town there is no such thing as privacy.' She looked away and said softly, 'And sometimes that's a good thing.'

'Anyway, once you're satisfied that Watson is as fine as fine can be, apart from a rather sore throat, which I'm sure can be soothed with the application of foods such as ice cream, jelly and custard, you might want to see the present I've brought you.' Dex indicated Iris as he spoke.

Bub had a good look at Watson's throat and finished her observations before turning to face Iris. The woman smiled brightly, taking both of Iris's hands in her own. She sighed and nodded slowly.

'You've brought me a paediatrician.' She ignored Dex and looked directly into Iris's eyes. 'How wonderful that you're here, darl.' The words were so heartfelt, so sincere that Iris was quite moved by them. 'First we were blessed with Melissa, who has been so wonderful for the female community, and now we have you— someone to look after our gorgeous children.' Bub squeezed Iris's hands before letting them go. 'Welcome.' And in the next instant Iris found herself being embraced warmly by the woman who so obviously ran this hospital.

'Er…thank you.'

Bub let her go and then started fussing around Watson's bed, straightening sheets and plumping pillows as she spoke. 'Now, I know you're only here for six months—a great pity Joss couldn't talk you into staying longer but perhaps you'll end up like Melissa and find yourself a nice young man and settle down here for good.'

'Uh…' Iris was taken aback by Bub's words. She tried to think of a polite way of saying that such a suggestion was absolutely ludicrous and the last thing on her mind. 'Well, it's a nice offer and definitely something to consider.'

'Good.'

Dex was momentarily puzzled. Obviously Bub didn't realise Iris was already married. He waited for Iris to set the other woman straight.

'But—' Iris felt compelled to continue '—I've already secured another appointment at the end of my six months here.'

At her words, Iris felt all eyes on her. Watson's, his mother's, Bub's and most of all Dex's.

'Where are you going?' Dex asked calmly.

'The children's hospital in Melbourne.' A

moment of silence followed her announcement and she wondered what she'd done wrong. She was only here for six months. This was just a job and one that not only afforded her the opportunity to get out of Sydney but which would look good on her résumé, thereby securing her the job she was really after.

'Oh.' Bub was the first to speak. 'Well, we wouldn't want to stand in the way of a fancy job in the city but perhaps there's still hope that you'll meet someone and decide to stay for longer.' She looked over at Dex. 'Turn on the charm, boy. Be nice. Make Iris so happy she doesn't want to leave.'

'But…' Dex was clearly confused. Wasn't Iris already married? Perhaps it was her husband who didn't want to stay in Didja any longer than six months. Rather than point out the obvious to Bub, he decided to simply turn the situation into a light-hearted moment. 'What would you like me to do, boss? Propose right now?' Even though the woman was married, he added silently.

Bub looked at him and smiled, the previous mood broken, to be replaced by one of joviality.

'Why not? Start how you mean to finish,' Bub added jokingly.

In a light-hearted and teasing manner, Dex immediately dropped to one knee and took Iris's hands in his. 'Iris Tennant, will you marry me?'

Iris glared at him for a second as though he'd grown an extra head. 'No!'

Dex shrugged, stood up again and looked at Bub. 'Can't say I didn't try,' he remarked, and winked at Watson and his mother, who were laughing. Then he glanced at Iris, a little confused as to why she didn't simply tell them that she was already hitched and that agreeing to marry him would only lead to a bigamy charge.

Instead, Iris looked around the room, even at the elderly woman who was dozing two beds up from Watson's. She shook her head slowly. 'You're all stark raving mad.'

After her first week in Didja, Iris sat out in the courtyard, which was situated behind the apartments.

'More wine?' Melissa asked, the two women enjoying the opportunity to simply sit down and catch up.

Iris shook her head. 'I'm fine, thanks.'

'So…your first week in the outback. How did it go?'

'Busy. So many children and they're all in need of a lot of attention.'

'That's how I felt after my first week. So many women needing help, needing attention, needing another female simply to talk to. It can get very lonely for the women and children out here.'

Iris nodded. 'It's interesting, though. Different and interesting.'

'Challenging,' Melissa agreed. She took a sip of her wine and relaxed more into the chair. 'I'm glad the boys went to the pub tonight. They can drink a few beers with their friends, play a game or two of pool and break up a fight.'

'Male bonding.' Iris nodded and Melissa chuckled.

'Exactly. And in turn we get to sit here and relax in peace and quiet, sharing a nice bottle of red. I'm really glad you agreed to come to Didja, Iris. It's nice having you here.'

'You're not going to try and convince me to stay longer?'

Melissa raised her eyebrows at that statement. 'What makes you ask that? Have you been pressured?' She took another sip of her wine.

'Only a bit. Dex proposed to me.'

Shocked, Melissa nearly spat her mouthful all over the place. Instead, she swallowed and then started coughing. Iris patted her on the back.

'Sorry. Should have picked my time better before imparting that piece of information.'

'What? When?' Melissa kept coughing.

'My first day here. He was only joking, I know that, but still…' She shrugged. 'It was rather startling.' And sort of nice and flattering, and for some reason she hadn't been able to stop thinking about it. In fact, throughout the week she'd caught herself sneaking glances at Dex, thinking about him and wondering what the look on his face would have been like if she'd said yes?

'Does he know about your husband?' Melissa had recovered now.

'He knows Tennant is my married name but apart from you and Joss, no-one knows about my past.'

'Pasts are a tricky thing. Unless your past affects your future, it should stay in the past.' Melissa smiled warmly at her friend. 'You've been through so much. Coped with so much. You're an inspiration to me, Iris.'

Iris smiled, accepting her friend's warm words. Then she paused for a second before asking, 'And no-one's said anything about my clothes?'

'What you wear is your business. If you want to wear long-sleeved shirts and trousers, then you do it. No one needs to know why.'

The scars on her arms, upper legs and torso were something she'd had to live with on a daily basis. They were also a constant reminder of the tragedy she'd lived through, of fighting that fire, of losing her husband and almost losing her own life.

'It's just out here, in the heat, people might wonder why I'm rugged up like a polar bear.'

'You're a strong woman, Iris. You're a survivor—in more ways than one. I like to surround myself with emancipated women and you are definitely one of them. If you're comfortable, why worry what other people think?'

'I'm so self-conscious about the scars. Still.' The words were said softly. 'I had thought that as time went on, as the red angriness started to fade from the affected areas, I'd be able to cope better.'

Melissa could feel her friend's pain. 'All I know is I'm glad you didn't die. I remember sitting by your bed in the burns unit night after night after night, hoping and praying that you'd live. And you did.'

Tears filled Melissa's eyes and Iris felt a wave of her own coming on as her friend continued speaking such heart-felt words.

'Physical scars you may still have but...' She reached over and touched Iris's hand. 'But you're still here. I've lost so many people, had them taken away from me. I'm just grateful you weren't one of them.' She sniffed and sat back, pulling a tissue from her pocket. 'I'm also glad you've come to Didja. I don't care if it's only for six months. I don't care if it's to get away from Sydney or because it helped secure you a job in Melbourne. You're here. I'm glad you're going to be here for my wedding, to get to know my wonderful Joss as well as my crazy brother.'

'Well…' Iris sniffed and pulled herself together. 'The crazy-brother part I could probably do without.'

Melissa sat back and laughed, before blowing her nose. 'He is a bit full on is Dex but underneath he's like a hurt little boy. He's finally starting to let me into his life, to open up, and it's fantastic. Still, he covers so much up with nonchalance and laughter.'

'And on-the-spot proposals,' Iris added.

'Yes.' Both women laughed.

'What's so funny?' a male voice said from behind them, and they both turned to see the man in question, as well as Melissa's fiancé, walking towards them.

'You two are back early.' Melissa accepted a sensual kiss from Joss. 'What? No fights tonight?'

'Nope.' Dex sank into a chair next to Iris. Joss stood behind Melissa, his hands protectively on her shoulders. 'Carto wasn't there so Bluey had no one to pick a fight with.'

'Wow. A Friday night in Didja with no fight to break up? Is that a first?' Melissa asked.

'Remember the first fight you had to assist me with at the pub?' Joss asked his fiancée, his blue eyes twinkling in the early evening light.

Melissa laughed and nodded. 'Do I ever.'

Dex groaned. 'Don't.'

Iris picked up on the amused tension. 'What happened?'

'Carto and Bluey got into their usual argument about football and started swinging punches,' Joss began.

'Don't.' Dex hung his head and shook it. Iris was now more intrigued than ever.

'Dex, being the strong, virile man that he is,' Joss continued, 'decided to break it up.'

'He was so macho,' Melissa teased her brother. 'Standing between the two men. Telling them to stop fighting.'

'Yeah, really macho.' Joss started to laugh. 'Until Bluey accidentally punched Dex instead of Carto.'

'I hate you both,' Dex murmured, and looked at

Iris. She was smiling brightly, her green eyes alive with anticipation and interest. Her hair was pulled back in its usual long single plait and she again wore the long cotton clothing which he was sure hid such a gorgeous, curvaceous figure. Still, the image she presented right now was…captivating. Didn't she have any idea just how stunning she was?

'He was out cold for a good thirty seconds,' Melissa said, grinning at her brother.

'And there we have it. Embarrassment is complete.' Everyone laughed and Dex took a little bow. 'Thank you both very much. You may go now,' he announced.

Joss patted Melissa's shoulders. 'We're being dismissed. Let's go.'

'Oh, right.' Melissa stood.

'It's been such a hectic week, we've hardly had two moments alone together,' Joss said by way of parting.

Before Iris could open her mouth and ask them both to stay, so she didn't end up out here alone with Dex, both Melissa and Joss had disappeared through the rear sliding door into Melissa's apartment.

Almost instantly, the atmosphere between the two who were left outside started to become uncomfortable. Iris had made sure that she hadn't been alone with Dex since they'd walked around at the fair last weekend. Spending time with him, one on one, only brought more awareness of just how good-looking the man really was. She didn't want to like him. She didn't want to be attracted to him and one way to avoid such a thing was never to be alone with him.

Now here they were, sitting outside beneath a cloudless starry sky. Both, she presumed, slightly touched by the effects of alcohol and yet both completely alert to the other person. It was an odd sensation but even without looking at him Iris could feel him breathing, could sense the rise and fall of his chest, could feel his presence surrounding her.

'So…' Dex was first to break the silence. 'Good week?'

'Yes. Thank you. How about yours?'

Dex leaned back in the chair and considered it for a moment. 'Let's see, I've done a busy clinic every day, had three emergencies come in for A and E care, managed to talk Melissa into doing my house calls for me, annoyed Joss, teased Bub and proposed to a beautiful woman. All in all…a pretty average week.'

He stretched his arms up above his head, the

cotton T-shirt he wore rising up slightly, the waistband of his shorts dipping slightly, leaving Iris with a glimpse of firm, muscled torso. A smattering of dark hair swirled around his navel and she found it difficult to avert her gaze. The last man she'd had such an overwhelming attraction to had ended up being her husband, so the only thing she could do was to ignore whatever it was she felt for her new colleague and never allow it to overwhelm her!

She forced herself to look away, turning her head and lifting her eyes to look out at where the land met the horizon, the tops of trees in silhouette. It was very relaxing. The wine had also been relaxing. What was annoying her now was the man beside her, who was still twisting from side to side, his arms still above his head, his body still on display for her to see.

'So an average week for you includes proposing to someone?'

Dex's answer was to chuckle and the sound washed over her, soothing some of those jagged nerves. He was trying to be nice, she knew that, and he couldn't know of the unwanted feelings he was stirring up within her.

He moaned as he stretched and then lowered

his arms. 'Man, my shoulders are tight. How are yours?'

Iris was surprised by the question and accidentally broke her resolve to not look at him. 'Fine.'

'Pity. I was hoping if yours were tight, too, we could help each other out.' He looked at her and grinned. 'You know…sort of an I'll massage your shoulders if you massage mine kind of deal. Purely platonic. Purely professional. I just have knots in my trapezius I can't reach.'

Iris bristled. The last thing she wanted was to be touched—by anyone. 'Well, my muscles are fine, thank you very much, and I'm sure you'll have no difficulty of finding someone to relieve your muscular aches and pains. Just ask one of those lovely ladies who were impatiently standing in line to kiss you last weekend.'

Dex watched as Iris shifted in her seat and couldn't believe he'd made her uncomfortable. It certainly hadn't been his intention to offend so what had he done now? He hadn't kissed her. He hadn't proposed to her. All he'd done was hint at getting her to massage his shoulders because they were sore…and because usually his charm worked on almost everyone he met. Almost. His new colleague, however, appeared very standoffish and it made him wonder what had happened in her past to make her that way.

When he'd tried to link arms with her at the fair last weekend, she'd been as stiff as a board yet trying very hard to be polite and keep him at a distance. When he'd attempted to kiss her…well, even though she'd shocked him by slapping him across the cheek, it had brought a smile to his face every time he'd thought of it. She had spirit and she intrigued him yet Dex was picking up a strong sensation that she wanted to keep a firm distance away, not only from him but from everyone else in the town as well.

She hadn't mentioned her marriage or anything to do with her husband during the past week, not that he'd had the chance to have any conversations with her. Every time he'd walked into the kitchenette in the clinic, if he'd found Iris in there on her own, she'd quickly excused herself and disappeared into her consulting room. Unable to ask her directly, Dex had been so interested he'd checked her résumé and discovered she was a widow.

It had helped him to fill in a few gaps and explained why sometimes, when he'd been watching her, he'd sensed a deep loneliness about her. Yet at other times, like this evening when she'd been around Melissa, he'd seen her laughing brightly, her eyes sparkling as though she didn't have a care in the world.

However, despite the different sides of Iris he'd managed to glimpse so far, the one he liked best was when she'd been watching him stretch. He hadn't intentionally stretched his muscles to show off his body—he stretched his muscles because they were tense. He'd been out helping a mate put up a back fence yesterday afternoon and his muscles were sore. He'd stretched—and Iris had looked.

What Dex hadn't expected was that he'd liked her visual caress more than he'd care to admit. The woman had plagued his thoughts quite a bit during this past week and he wasn't used to that at all. He didn't mind the fact that he was interested in her but he was wary that he'd had a difficult time wiping her from his mind, especially at night-time.

When he'd discovered she was indeed available, he'd been secretly pleased but then he'd started asking himself why. Why should he be pleased? Iris was just another colleague. Just another woman and a woman who appeared to have quite a few things she needed to work out in her personal life. He knew Didja would help her—it was the magic of the outback—but as far as he was concerned, he needed to keep his distance from the gorgeous woman sitting beside him. But for some strange reason thoughts of Iris persisted.

He wanted to ask her questions, to listen to her talk, to hear her laugh, to watch a smile play about her lips. It had been made abundantly clear to him that he was definitely attracted to her but he knew the attraction would never last. It never did. People changed. They moved on. And he had locked his heart away, determined it would never get hurt again.

Iris shifted in her chair again, putting her hand onto her wineglass as though getting ready to make her escape. Dex didn't want her to leave, not yet. He tried to think of the last thing she'd said. That's right, she'd made some comment about women standing in line for him.

'You do know that the women in that line weren't serious.'

'Pardon?' Iris raised an eyebrow at him. He'd sat there for a good minute or two not saying a thing and then just when she was about to leave, he threw out a comment like that!

'The women. The kissing. It didn't mean anything. It was just for a good cause.'

'To raise funds for an ambulance, and it was good that we succeeded in that cause. Joss has said the ambulance should be here in two months' time. However, I also remember a lot of those women getting quite impatient whilst waiting for you to kiss them, as well as a lot of them leaving the line when Bluey took his turn. Admit it, Dex. You're more than happy to have the women of this community salivating for you.'

He chuckled at her words. 'Charming image,' he murmured, which only seemed to make her angry.

Iris stood, wineglass forgotten in her haste to leave, and nearly jumped out of her skin when Dex stood too. She felt he was crowding her when in reality there was actually quite a bit of physical distance between them. 'You take nothing seriously,' she huffed. 'It's pointless trying to have a proper conversation with you.'

Dex stared at her, his words soft and clear. 'It's difficult trying to have *any* conversation with you.'

Iris glared at him. 'What does that mean?'

'It just means that during this past week, any time I walk into a room, you walk out of it. You're elusive, you're closed off and that's fine—to a point—but we're colleagues, Iris. This is a very small community. We're going to need to have some conversation at some point.'

'We're talking now.'

'And that's good, but during the week would be helpful, too.'

'I didn't walk out of the room when we had our business meeting.' Iris wasn't at all sure what to say, mainly because Dex was right. What she hadn't realised was that he'd not only noticed her keeping her distance from him but that he cared enough to comment on it. It appeared out here in the outback, there was no beating about the bush. Honesty reigned.

'That's not what I'm talking about and you know it. You're here for six months and that's great. Sure, we'd all love it if you stayed longer, mainly because the children of this community will benefit from having a specialist here, but that's beside the point.'

'Which is?'

'I don't go around proposing to women at the drop of a hat.' Dex looked down at the ground for a moment and Iris was surprised at the sincerity of his words. 'I wanted to apologise if I made you feel uncomfortable. It was a joke and now I realise a rather bad one.' He met her eyes, even though it was now rather dark and difficult to read her expression. 'At that time, I had no idea you were a widow.'

Iris stared at him, uncertain what to say, but he continued.

'I've been trying to apologise all week. I'm glad I finally got the opportunity.'

'How did you find out? Did you ask Melissa? Joss? Did you discuss me with them?'

She was still mad. Dex wasn't quite sure why. He'd made a mistake. He'd apologised. Those tactics had helped him through countless situations in the past and he wondered if he'd used up his 'charisma' quota for the day.

'No. Neither of them said a word.' He glanced away for a moment before meeting her gaze. 'I read your résumé. Your marital status was on there.'

'You did what? You don't think that's Joss's business? He does own the clinic after all. Isn't it his business who he hires and why?'

Dex frowned for a moment. Perhaps Iris didn't realise he was as much a financial partner in the clinic as Joss was. It was true that Joss had more of a flair for the day-to-day running and management side of things but where staffing was concerned, he had just as much right to read a résumé as Joss.

Right now, as he watched Iris he realised there was more going on than he'd initially realised.

'What your résumé didn't say was how your husband died or how much pain you might have felt during the past four years or how deeply the whole situation had affected you.'

'No, it doesn't, so stop digging around, Dex. Stop trying to get to know me. I know your type. You're a love 'em and leave 'em type of guy. You hold yourself aloof, not only from relationships with women but from relationships with everyone. You forget that I know Melissa. I was the friend she leaned on when her parents died. I was the friend who supported her when she went looking for her birth mother. I was the friend she confided in when she discovered she had a brother, and I was the friend who passed her the tissues when you initially refused to see her.

'Now, I know you're trying to make good by getting to know her and I hope you do because she is one amazing woman who was there for me when I needed her most.' Iris's voice cracked on the last words. She hated Dex for making her feel so vulnerable.

Dex instinctively put out a hand to offer comfort but she shrugged it away.

'Don't touch me. I don't like being touched.'

'Why? People should be touched. It's part of the healing process…and it's something I'm learning myself.'

'You? You who are surrounded by women all the time?'

Dex made a point of looking around him. 'I only see one woman.' For some reason he had a burning need to get through to her, to let her see he wasn't the Casanova she thought he was. 'Look, I know I'm not perfect and I don't profess to be, but I have issues, too. Melissa's probably told you I haven't spoken to my parents in over two years. I had no idea I was adopted until I received Melissa's first letter. My parents never told me, so for thirty-one years I firmly believed I was their son. I believed my younger brother and sister were my siblings. I was lied to and I know all about cutting yourself off and not wanting anyone to touch you—whether it be physical or emotional. You can be surrounded by people and still be quite alone simply because you don't let any of them touch you. Not the real you. Not the person you've hidden away inside.'

'Why are you telling me this?'

Dex took a step away from her and raked a hand

through his hair. 'I don't know. Perhaps it's because I don't like it that you don't like me.' He shrugged and smiled. 'I guess I'm used to being liked but I also know I'm not perfect. I've been hurt in love before. I've been betrayed by the ones I love. I also had an accident a few weeks ago—almost a month ago now. I lost a lot of blood but thankfully Melissa was there to help me out. Still, at times like that, at those really dark, dark times, it makes a person think. It made me realise that I couldn't keep running from my problems.'

'You think I'm running?'

Dex spread his arms wide, indicating the surroundings. 'You're in Didja. Nine times out of ten, people come here to escape from something.'

'And tell me, Dr Freud. What am I escaping from?'

Dex shrugged, not caring that she was still mad at him. If being mad helped him to get to know her better, then for the moment, so be it. 'My first guess would be whatever happened to your husband. It must have been a traumatic death to leave you with such deep scars.'

Iris's mouth went dry and she started to tremble at his words. Her vision had blurred a little due to the tears she was trying to control. She felt her knees begin to buckle and she clutched wildly for the support of one of the chairs but couldn't find one. Dex immediately put out his hand to support her and she grabbed it. 'How?' Her words were barely above a whisper, her body trembling with disbelief. 'How did you know about my scars?'

CHAPTER FOUR

DEX was astounded, not only at the complete emotional switch around but at the anguish and pain in her words.

He'd only been employing a bit of basic psychology but it appeared he'd literally hit the nail on the head. Iris was breathing rather fast, her eyes wide with confusion as she looked up at him. The trembling was getting worse and Dex tried to ease her back into the chair but it appeared she couldn't move.

Dex wasn't sure exactly what was happening or what he'd actually said to bring on this reaction from her, but what he knew right then was that she needed him—and it felt so good to be needed. His birth mother hadn't wanted him, Catherine hadn't needed him and his parents had lied to him. Yes. It felt good that he could do something to help someone else. Dex gathered Iris into his arms, showing her that he did indeed care about her.

'I've got you. Shh. It's OK. Lean on me.'

Iris closed her eyes, her mind whirring out of control with so many different emotions. How on earth had Dex figured out about her scars? One minute she was cross with him because he was so good-looking, so dynamic and was affecting her way too much and the next she was in his arms, trembling and unable to control the feelings coursing through her.

He'd said he hadn't talked to Melissa or Joss about her past. He'd read her résumé and discovered she was a widow. How had he put two and two together and come up with four? Were her scars obvious? Could he feel them beneath her clothes?

'I'm always so careful. I always make sure I'm covered. People stare and then they…they…' She hiccuped as though trying to control tears that were threatening to escape.

'They what?' he encouraged softly. So that was it. Iris had scars—physical scars on her body. It was why she dressed the way she did, to cover the scars. When he'd mentioned scars before, he'd been speaking metaphorically, not literally. His heart swelled with compassion for this woman who had obviously been through something extremely traumatic if she actually had physical scars.

He only hoped she'd let him help her. He knew she wouldn't think he was the first choice when it came to finding a reliable friend to confide in but he wanted to help because this woman, this unique and remarkable woman, was affecting him in a way no other woman had. Not even Catherine.

'People become sympathetic. Poor Iris. Look at her scars.' Bitterness tinged her words and Dex wanted to wipe it all away, to let her know that it didn't matter, but he really had no idea what to say. He didn't want to sound patronising, he didn't want to preach about something he knew nothing about, so he simply stood there, holding her, letting her lean on him.

'Or they want to know how it happened. They want to talk about it, to help me, when all I want to do is forget about it and I can't. I can't.' She broke on the last two words and the tears started to flow. Deep tears filled with complete anguish. She buried her face into Dex's chest and sobbed. He held her tight, rubbing his hands lightly up and down her back in a soothing manner.

He could feel the slight roughness of her skin through the shirt. She had scars on her back. She said she had them on her arms and he wondered just how much of her body had been injured. His medical mind worked quickly to come up with possible scenarios for such extensive scarring and he finally settled on burns. Scars like this could only have been caused by fire. He'd been an A and E specialist for so long, he'd seen and treated everything.

He would patch people up, get them breathing again, get them sorted out. He would resuscitate and intubate, he would debride and bandage. He would do his job and then send them on their way to the ward or to a specialist or to Theatre. It was the type of medicine he'd always liked— fix 'em up and move 'em out. It had suited his personality of being in the thick of things but still holding himself apart. It was another after-effect of the lessons he'd learned with Catherine. Don't give too much of yourself, keep your heart well and truly locked away and you won't get hurt.

So that was what he'd done at the hospital. He'd been nice and polite to everyone. He'd joined in with jokes, he'd gone on dates but at no time had he ever made a serious commitment to anyone. He'd been like a leaf on the wind.

That had been until he'd come to Didja. The people of this community didn't allow doctors to treat them as numbers, or as just another patient. They were people in their own right and they demanded their doctors acknowledge that and get involved not only in the community but in other people's lives. Some of his closest friends were also his patients, which made the level of treatment at the Didja Clinic that of first-class quality.

Dex had changed a lot in the past two years. Even he could see it. Didja had been good for him and he'd come to realise that offering compassion, offering a listening ear, showing people he really cared could also go a long way in restoring them to full health.

It made him wonder what type of care Iris had received. Had her treating doctors viewed her as a person or just a number? Emotional wounds took far longer to heal than physical wounds, something he was well aware of himself. Had Iris been nurtured through her healing process? With the way she was sobbing now, he had his doubts.

Dex stopped rubbing her back, not wanting her to think he was being insensitive. He still held her close, though the tears were now starting to subside. He fished in his pocket for a handkerchief and pulled one out, getting it ready to offer.

'I want to forget about what happened,' she said softly, her words a little more controlled then before. 'I don't want to forget Tim but I want to forget what happened. I want the memory—the vivid, Technicolor memory—of that awful day to be wiped away.' Iris eased back, sniffing as she raised red-rimmed eyes to look at Dex.

'Tim was your husband?'

'Yes.'

'How long were you married?' His questions were soft and caring.

'Two years.' Iris swallowed and accepted the handkerchief he offered. She gave him an embarrassed smile. 'I must look a sight.'

Dex shrugged. 'Even if you do—and I'm not saying I agree with that statement—who's going to know?'

'You.' Iris eased from his arms and sat in the closest chair. 'I can't believe I had such an outburst.'

'I wouldn't call it an outburst as such.' Dex sat next to her, bringing his chair a little nearer.

'I would.'

Dex shook his head. 'Well, it was a fairly tame one.' He leaned back in the chair and looked up at the starry sky. 'When I found out I was adopted, after my parents confirmed the contents of Melissa's letter to be the truth, I had an outburst and it was nowhere near as sedate as yours.'

Iris was intrigued. 'What did you do?'

'I decided to wrap my very expensive Ferrari around a tree.'

'On purpose?'

Dex exhaled slowly. 'At the time, I wasn't sure. I was just so angry, so out of control that I wanted to get away from everyone and everything and so I drove. I just drove and drove, going faster around the corners, heading away from civilisation and everything it stood for. The power of the machine, the noise from the engine. I wanted it all to wipe out my thoughts, my feelings—and then I woke up in hospital.'

'You don't remember the accident?'

'No, but from the pictures Joss showed me of my car, which was literally wrapped around a tree, it's a complete miracle I survived.'

'You're lucky.'

'Lucky I survived or lucky I don't remember what happened?'

'Both.' Iris couldn't believe how nice, how understanding, how *human* Dex was being. Melissa had told her that there were more layers to him than just the surface ones and she couldn't believe he was letting her see them. Perhaps he felt compelled to share given that she'd all but soaked his T-shirt with her tears. 'But more that you don't remember.'

'Do you still have nightmares about the fire?' Again his tone was soft, caring and she even thought she detected a small hint of worry. Dex? Worried about someone other than himself?

Hang on. He'd said *fire*. He might have glimpsed her scars but he couldn't know every-thing. Iris frowned. 'How did you know—'

'About the fire?' He shrugged a nonchalant shoulder and smiled that gorgeous hundred-watt smile of his. 'I'm a man of hidden talents.'

'Lis and Jos—'

'Haven't said a word,' he quickly interrupted. 'They'd never betray a confidence.'

Iris's mind worked quickly. She remembered the way Dex had held her, the way he'd soothed, the way he'd gently stroked her back. Her eyes widened imperceptibly. Dex must have felt the scars. Through the thin cotton shirt, he would have been able to feel her skin and the angry dis-tortions left there from the burns. He'd touched her scars and then…then after that, she remem-bered him just holding her.

He'd felt how bad her scars were and been repulsed by them. Right now, he wasn't making any effort to touch her so that was obviously all there was to it. Whatever attraction she might have felt towards Dexter could now be forgotten because there was no way in the world this handsome, gorgeous man was going to want someone as physically scarred as she was, especially when he had no end of smooth-skinned women throughout the community throwing themselves at him.

'Of course they wouldn't,' she agreed. She'd momentarily forgotten that Dex was an A and E specialist and had no doubt come across his fair share of burns victims in the past.

'And neither will I. You have my professional word on that.'

'Thank you, Dex.' Iris stayed where she was, still unsure whether her legs would support her. 'So…you, uh, crashed your very expensive car and woke up in hospital. Then what?'

Dex could see she wanted to change the subject, to take the focus away from herself, and he was happy to oblige. He wanted Iris to be able to trust him, to talk to him, to let him help her through the grief she'd been repressing for far too long.

She'd no doubt grieved for her husband and the loss of his life, but she hadn't grieved for herself. Instead, after healing, she'd probably thrown herself back into work and forgotten that she had emotions that needed to be addressed as well.

He knew, because he'd been there…was *still* there in a way. He hadn't dealt with his feelings for his family, hadn't addressed the entire betrayal issue, and even now he didn't want to talk about it. He could, however, tell her about his crash, especially if it helped her to relax a little more.

'Uh…after I crashed the car that I'd worked day and night to pay off, Joss came to Perth to visit me in hospital.' Dex's words held a strong touch of brotherly love. 'He told me I was an idiot and a complete fool and that if I wanted to get out of town and away from everyone else I should move to Didja and help him out.'

'And so you moved here, put some space between you and your problems and became the local playboy.'

Dex laughed at her words. 'Local playboy? I don't think I've ever been called that before.'

'Probably not to your face, but isn't that what you are?'

'A playboy.' He mulled the word over, folding

his arms across his chest. 'If a playboy enjoys the company of beautiful and intelligent women, perhaps I am.'

'Do they need to be intelligent?'

Dex thought on this question for a moment. 'I think it helps if you want to have a decent conversation with them.'

'And do they need to be beautiful?'

'Ah, and there's a loaded question if ever I've heard one. I would have to say that there's beauty and then there's beauty—real beauty. The kind that radiates from deep within the soul.'

Iris was pleasantly surprised by his answer. 'Careful, Dex. I might start to think you're a romantic at heart.'

He uncrossed his arms and shifted in his seat, angling a little closer to her. 'And I might start to think you actually like me.'

'Well…' Iris edged to the end of the chair. 'We can't have that, now, can we,' she stated rhetorically as she stood, incredibly grateful that her legs were going to support her. 'I'd best go in. I have Saturday clinic tomorrow.' She picked up her wineglass and reached for Melissa's, which was near Dex.

'I've got it,' he said, and picked up both the

glass and the half-empty bottle. He sniffed the wine as they made their way over to Iris's rear sliding door. 'Smells like a good year.'

She stopped outside her apartment. 'Would you like a glass? I could get a fresh one.'

He shook his head. 'It's fine. Thanks.'

'Oh, I forgot you'd been to the pub earlier. Don't like mixing beer and wine?'

'Don't like mixing medication and alcohol is more to the point. Joss has me on another lot of antibiotics from the surgery I had a while ago.'

'That's right. I'd forgotten about that. You were involved in an accident at the mine or something like that?'

He nodded at her vague description of what had happened out at the Didja mine. 'The tyre of a mining truck exploded.'

'Really? Those trucks are enormous.'

'They are.'

'It's a miracle you weren't killed.'

'It is.' There was a hint of seriousness to those two words as though once again Dex was facing some deep emotional decisions.

'You had internal bleeding and gave your sister quite a scare.' She nodded. 'Melissa did give me more specific details but that was when I was in the middle of packing up to come here so things became a little hectic.'

'Lis fusses too much.'

'She's a nurturer and she's your sister. She loves you, Dex.'

'I know. I'm really starting to see that.'

'Caring for people is what Lis has done for so long.' Iris opened the door and went inside. Dex followed, placing the glass and wine bottle on the bench. He looked around the room and noticed Iris hadn't personalised the apartment in any way. The furniture that had been provided was all still in place but there were no books, no music, no pictures anywhere. If he needed a reminder that she didn't want to stay in town, this was it.

'And now she has Joss,' Dex added. 'He likes taking care of *her.*'

Iris smiled and Dex was momentarily stunned at the sight of her gorgeous twinkling eyes. No one would have guessed that not too long ago she'd been wrapped in his arms, crying. There were no tear stains on her face, no blotchy skin or red nose. Instead, she looked vibrant.

'I'm really pleased about that. I've never seen Lis so happy. She has a man who really loves her and the brother she's always wanted. I'm glad you agreed to meet her.'

'I am, too.' His words were spoken slowly and softly as though he'd given them a lot of thought, or was it that he'd given Melissa a lot of thought? Iris knew things hadn't been too rosy when Melissa had first arrived in Didja but now everything really was coming up roses…or whatever they grew out here. 'She is sort of wonderful.'

Iris slowly shook her head.

'What?' he prompted when she didn't say anything.

'You.'

'What about me?'

'Tonight… I don't know, you're just…'

'Charming? Gallant? Incredibly witty?'

'I was going to say you're breaking the stereotypes I had assigned to you.'

'Ah…haven't you ever heard that you shouldn't judge a book by its cover?'

'Yes. I've also heard that a leopard doesn't change its spots.'

Dex chuckled. 'I've heard that too.' He walked towards the door, sliding it open, trying not to wince as his trapezius muscles made themselves known yet again.

'Put a heat pack on it.'

'Pardon?'

'Your muscles.'

'Oh.' He looked sheepish. 'I thought you hadn't seen the wince.'

Iris nodded. 'I did. I'm guessing you're not as macho as you make out, either.'

Dex stepped outside. 'I'm a lonely, wimpy little boy on the inside,' he said, and Iris was surprised at the seriousness evident both on his face and in his words.

'And on the outside?'

'I'm a rugged superhero.' He flexed his arms, his biceps rippling very nicely beneath his T-shirt. A second later he dropped his arms and rolled his shoulders, massaging one of them with his hand. 'Seriously, though, I wear a mask. Just like everyone else. Even you.'

Iris wasn't sure what to say to that so she said nothing.

'See you tomorrow, Dr Tennant,' he continued. 'Sleep sweet.' And with that he disappeared into the night.

Iris was up bright and early the next morning, mainly because she'd found it difficult to sleep.

To know that Dex's apartment backed onto hers, to know that he was on the other side of the wall was something of which she was acutely aware.

During the week she'd spent in Didja, she'd occasionally heard noises coming from his apartment but after last night, after she'd seen a completely different side to Dexter Crawford—a side she most definitely liked—she'd actually found herself listening.

Last night, he'd not only shown her compassion, he'd shown her he had far more depth than she'd credited him with. Dex had held her in his arms, had been supportive rather than inquisitive. As she'd lain in her bed, the ceiling fan whirring above, she'd replayed the entire conversation, the entire scene in her head and it was only then she had realised her own mistake. Embarrassment had swamped her as she'd remembered Dex mentioning her scars.

'He was speaking metaphorically, you twit,' she told her reflection as she dried her hair. She turned the hairdryer off and brushed the long locks back so she could plait it and keep it out of the way. 'He didn't know about your physical scars.' She glanced at her upper arms as she spoke, the stretched, distorted skin mocking her.

Now Dex knew. He knew she was scarred. He'd felt the unevenness on her back and he'd been repulsed by what he'd inadvertently touched. She didn't blame him. She was repulsed herself. Iris flicked the completed plait down her back and stood straight, looking at herself. The white bra with tiny pink flowers was a complete contrast against the scars on her upper torso. One was pretty, the other was ugly.

She turned sideways to look at the marks on her back. The skin was worse here, more raised, more prominent if someone were to touch them. Someone like Dex. Iris raised her hands to her face, covering her eyes, unable to look any more. She knew the contour of every mark, she felt the emotional pain and anguish every time she looked at them.

They were a constant reminder of how she'd failed to save her husband's life. The cruel twist of fate that had allowed her to live whilst Tim had suffered and died. She'd been there. She'd watched him die and there had been nothing she could do. The firefighters had smothered the flames that had caught her clothing, they'd wrapped her up and carried her out. Her last conscious sight had been that of Tim, lying there, surrounded by fire and thick smoke…dead.

Sniffing, she raised her head and forced herself to concentrate on taking deep breaths. She was due at the clinic in ten minutes and she needed to pull herself together. Work was wonderful. Work helped and at least today she wouldn't be having to avoid Dex all the time. It was Saturday. She was the doctor on call and he was off…somewhere, no doubt with a string of pretty bimbos following him as though he were the Pied Piper.

Ignoring her scars by not looking at them, by pretending they weren't there, Iris blew her nose and then finished dressing. After a quick cup of tea and a piece of toast, she headed to the little hospital.

'Good morning, Iris,' Bub said as Iris walked into the room. 'Here to do a quick ward round?'

Iris scanned the ten beds. Three had patients in them. 'A *very* short round by the looks of it.'

Bub waved away her words. 'Oh, we may be small in numbers but we're big on the need to chat.' The experienced nursing sister leaned closer and said in a stage whisper, 'Just don't let Mr Bloffwith get started on his new irrigation system. He'll have you there for hours.'

'Right. Good. Thanks for the tip.' Iris looked around, feeling a little bereft. She was used to conducting ward rounds with at least twenty other people. Surgeons, registrars, interns, medical students, nursing staff, dieticians, physiotherapists. She was also used to having far more than three patients to contend with. Still, as Bub conducted her to each bed, it was done in a highly professional manner. Things may be more relaxed out here but they were certainly efficient.

Once the ward round was completed—and Mr Bloffwith's new irrigation system chatter neatly diverted—Iris thanked Bub before making her way to the clinic. As it was her first weekend on call, Joss had come over to open everything up and to make sure she knew what was going on.

'Areva, our incredible receptionist, doesn't work Saturdays. So it's just you and the patients. We work the weekends on a first come, first served basis so you'll find that some people will get here as early as possible and sometimes they're even waiting outside the doors when you open them.' He indicated the empty waiting room. 'Thankfully, today that isn't the case.'

Iris nodded. 'I'm sure I'll be fine, Joss.'

'I'm sure you will, too. Lis speaks very highly of you and I have to say that during the past week, I've been incredibly impressed.'

'Thank you.' Iris was pleased to hear such a glowing report from her new boss. 'Now, why don't you go and find your fiancée and spend some time with her?'

Joss grinned widely and Iris could see just why Melissa had been attracted to the handsome general surgeon. 'What a brilliant idea. I think I'll go and do exactly what the doctor's ordered.' He took a few steps away before turning back. 'Oh, and if you need any help, if emergencies come in, contact Bub and she'll get one of us here to help assist you.'

'Right. Will do. Now go. Have fun.'

Joss grinned widely and nodded before almost sprinting from the clinic. Iris was left alone within seconds and she walked to the front door of the clinic, checking outside to ensure there really wasn't anyone waiting.

With no patients to see, she decided to switch the kettle on and then make sure her consulting room was set up and ready to go. She did this. Still no patients. She made herself a cup of tea and drank it—slowly. Still no patients. Was it usually like this? What was the point in having a weekend clinic if no one was going to come?

She sat in the waiting room…and waited, scanning a few of the magazines, flipping through others and not reading a word. She checked outside the door again, looking up and down the street. A few people waved but no one came in. Iris returned to her consulting room, unable to believe that for the first time in…well, she couldn't remember when, she was actually bored.

Sighing, she allowed her thoughts to wander and oddly enough they turned immediately to her handsome single colleague. She wondered what Dex was really doing today. What did most of the townsfolk do on a weekend when there was no Australia Day fair, when there were no fundraisers to attend? Surely they'd have sports out here. They'd have to or else the lot of them would go completely barmy.

Did Dex play Australian Rules football? Or did he prefer cricket? Maybe soccer was his game. He obviously did something athletic because when she'd been held tightly in his arms the previous evening, she'd noted the firmness of those muscles as he'd held her close. His chest had also been nice and taut beneath his T-shirt and she doubted there was an ounce of flab on him. Pure, solid muscle…and what delicious-looking muscle it was.

She wondered if she'd ever get the chance to really feel it. To run her fingertips over his biceps, to caress the solid six-pack of his abdomen, the broadness of his shoulders. She also wanted to plunge her fingers into his dark, unruly hair, to feel the texture between her finger and thumb. He had the most alluring voice, his tones rich and deep. His brown eyes, so incredibly expressive. And his mouth…

Oh, yes. Dex Crawford really was one in a million and she could quite easily drown simply by looking at him. Iris's eyelids fluttered closed as she pictured him, so clearly. She sighed, long and slowly, as she leaned back in her chair.

'Something I can help you with?' Deep, husky, masculine tones washed over her.

Iris sat bolt upright in her chair, her eyelids snapping open instantly. Dex was standing in her doorway—lounging in her doorway—and the look on his face said that he was more than willing to offer her his services for…whatever she'd been thinking about!

CHAPTER FIVE

'DEX!'

'Iris.'

'What are you…?' She couldn't believe how fast her heart was pounding in her chest, how breathless she felt and how she was so glad she was sitting down as she felt her body begin to tremble. She'd been sitting there, thinking about the man who was now before her, and she'd been thinking such tantalising things, she was sure she was also blushing.

'Doing here?' He shrugged and sauntered into the room. 'Just thought I'd stop by and see if you needed any help.'

'Uh… No, thanks, because, as you can see, all is quiet on the western front.'

He smiled at her words as he sat down opposite her. She wished he wouldn't. She wished he'd up and leave, go as far away from the clinic as he could in order to give her peace of mind and a lot more breathing space than currently existed between them. She also wished he wouldn't smile at her like that! Didn't the man have any idea just how irresistible he was?

Of course he did. That was why he was here. He needed her to fall for him just like all the other women in the town. He needed to know she'd be definitely joining the line if there was another kissing booth in the future. He had an ego the size of Uluru and she'd do well to remember it.

She *had* to remember it because if she started thinking about the man she'd been with last night, the man who had offered compassion and comfort, the man who had been anything but a playboy, then she'd start to give in to the feelings he still managed to evoke just by being this close to her.

'You don't need to be here.' Her words were a little more brisk than she'd intended. 'It's your day off, Dex. I'm sure you have better things to do than to hang around this place.'

'Maybe I like *this place.*'

Iris raised her eyebrows at that. 'Well, there's nothing going on clinic-wise. It's as dead as a dodo.'

Dex looked at her thoughtfully for a moment then clapped his hands together and rubbed them with mock excitement. 'A quiet western front and dead dodos. This place is sounding more interesting than the pub on a Friday night.' And Iris Tennant was a woman who was somehow continuing to interest him.

Last night, ensconced safely back in his own apartment, a heat pack on his shoulders, Dex had reflected on what he'd learned about his new colleague. A widow. Fire. Scarred body. If that wasn't some serious baggage she was carrying around, he didn't know what was. She may be stunning, she may have a sharp and intelligent mind, but he knew it wasn't his job to help her work through that baggage.

After Catherine, Dex had firmly decided he wasn't capable of having a fully involved, adult relationship. He'd messed up badly all those years ago, and that was the reason why he'd adopted the type of lifestyle that avoided emotional commitment. Serious romantic relationships would only lead to pain and heartbreak and it was a road he wasn't prepared to travel again.

Iris, however, *had* travelled that road. She'd met a man, married him and then suffered a great tragedy. It was clear she was still grieving for her husband and as such, Dex could see that her own dreams would remain, largely, unfulfilled. No.

He wasn't the person to help her through this. Whilst he was positive the community of Didja would help heal Iris, *he* wasn't the man for the job. She was a colleague. He would be helpful, friendly but that was all.

At least, that was the vow he'd made last night and so why he'd felt compelled to come to the clinic this morning to see how she was getting on was as much of a surprise to him as it had apparently been to her. What was it about the woman sitting opposite him that continually drew him in? He wished he knew because perhaps if he could put his finger on it, he'd be able to do something more proactive to lessen its effects.

In fact, he should do as she'd suggested and leave her to do her job. He should get up. Mumble something about just making sure she was all settled in and then leave. Being around Iris only made him want to know more, to breathe in that scent of hers, which was filled with sweetness and light, to watch as her emerald eyes sparked with annoyance as they were doing now. She wanted him gone. He shouldn't argue with that.

Still, he didn't move.

'So…is there something you needed? Wanted?

Anything I can help you with?' Iris decided the direct approach was her only hope to get him gone.

Dex's mouth twitched with amusement at her words. 'Now, there are three very loaded questions. Is there something I need?' As his rich brown gaze skimmed over her upper torso, Iris tried not to gasp at the visual caress, her heart rate, which had only just started to return to normal, picking up pace again. 'Is there something I want?' His gaze focused on her mouth and her traitorous lips parted with quivering anticipation.

Dex leaned forward so his elbows were on the desk, his gaze now flicking between her eyes and her lips. 'Is there anything *you* can help me with?' The words were soft, husky and exceedingly intimate. 'Oh, Iris.' Her name was like a whispered caress on his lips. 'I do believe there is.'

Iris swallowed. Once. Twice. Still she seemed to be incapable of speech. Third time lucky. She sucked in a deep breath and forced herself to speak. 'And what might that be?' Her eyes widened imperceptibly as she heard her own voice. Why had those words come out sounding like a husky invitation for him to join her in an early morning tryst?

Silence reigned between them, their bodies

appearing to have a completely different conversation to the one being spoken aloud. Finally, Dex spoke.

'Dinner. Tonight. Stiggie's.'

It took but a moment for his words to penetrate the haze he'd created around them. Was he asking her out? Was he demanding she go with him? To dinner? As in a date?

These thoughts helped Iris to snap out of the bubble she'd been in as her temper began to rise. Dex was a player. She had to keep remembering that. Add to that fact that he no doubt felt sorry for her now that he'd discovered her traumatic past. He'd asked her out to dinner last weekend without knowing anything about her and now that he knew far more than she'd planned on revealing, it was nothing more than a pity invite. A sour taste rose in her mouth but she ignored it. What did it matter that she found this man attractive? Nothing, because she knew, deep down in her heart, that he would never find her so.

Without moving and still holding his gaze, she said quietly but firmly, 'No.'

Dex didn't seem to be offended. He leaned back, though, putting some much-needed distance between them. He crossed his legs, one ankle resting on the opposite knee, his whole attitude displaying nonchalance. 'Why not?'

'Why?' she countered.

'I told you last week at the fair that we'd go to Stiggie's on Saturday night and sample the food in his restaurant.'

'That's right. You *told* me. You never asked me, Dex. In fact, you still haven't asked me.'

'All right.' He sat up straighter, squared his shoulders and looked her directly in the eyes. She wished he hadn't because it was his eyes that made her want to forget everything and to completely throw caution to the wind.

'Iris, would you like to go with me to Stiggie's tonight to sample the delicious food at his restaurant?'

Iris smiled politely at him. 'Well, Dex. What a sweet offer and how nice of you to ask. Unfortunately, if I'd known sooner, I wouldn't have made other plans.'

'Plans?' His frown was real and it was clear Dex wasn't used to being turned down. Iris was pleased with herself. Other women in this community may not have willpower when it came to their leading bachelor boy, but she certainly did. 'What plans?'

'That, Dr Crawford,' Iris said, standing as she heard the sound of someone actually coming in the front door of the clinic, 'is none of your business.'

With that, she walked straight past him, out of her consulting room towards the waiting room. Dex leaned back in the chair and shook his head. What was that all about? He had thought Iris would be happy to go out to dinner, to meet some of the community at Stiggie's. Sure, Saturday night was like 'date night' in this town but that didn't have to mean a thing. They were colleagues. He hoped they could become friends. It had nothing at all to do with the fact that he hadn't been able to stop thinking about her last night.

She'd obviously had such terrible things happen to her, had gone through so much, was no doubt still dealing with a lot of the emotional fallout from such trauma, but she was here, she was dealing with it, she was being strong. Even though he kept telling himself that Iris Tennant wasn't his type, he couldn't help but want to be around her.

Deciding to come and help her in the clinic had been a strictly professional decision. He was helping his new colleague settle in. What he hadn't expected was to find the clinic empty and the woman who had plagued his dreams last night sitting in her chair, relaxed and happy, a smile on her face as she'd sighed with utter longing.

Had she been thinking about her husband?

He swallowed at the thought, wondering at the sudden stirring of jealousy within his gut. No. Ridiculous. He couldn't be jealous. He didn't do jealousy. He held himself aloof from those sorts of emotions. He immediately pushed the thought away, telling himself sternly that Iris was only in Didja for six months. She was a colleague. His relationship with her should be one of pure professionalism and mild friendship. Nothing more. Really, fighting his attraction to her should be the least of his problems.

'Dex!'

Iris's shout from the waiting room was tinged with urgency. He was on his feet in a split second and bolted to the waiting room. It was only then he realised the noise level surrounding them. 'Something I can help you with?'

Those were the same words he'd said to her before but this time they held a completely different connotation. She was pleased he was calm, that although she could see his eyes taking in the entire situation, he still outwardly remained calm.

'Sorry to yell. Didn't mean to startle you.' Iris

glanced at him as she took a five-year-old boy from his mother. The child was screaming so loudly she thought her eardrums might burst. 'Thought you might not have heard me otherwise.'

'Oh, I heard,' he remarked as he looked at the father, who was coming into the clinic holding another screaming child. 'Smitty?' Dex directed his comments to the father. 'What on earth's been happening at your place?'

Smitty shook his head. 'Wouldn't believe me if I told ya.' He smiled, his white teeth shining out against his dark skin.

'Try,' Dex encouraged as he followed Iris, who was heading towards her consulting room. 'Maybe we should take them both straight to the hospital. Give us more room to move,' he suggested. He wasn't sure how Iris would take his suggestion. After all, officially she was the one in charge. Would she ignore him, tell him to mind his own business, or would she listen?

'Makes sense.' She veered off, the five-year-old still wailing like a banshee at the top of his lungs. 'I still have no idea what's happened.' She looked to Smitty for an answer and the man shook his head as they rounded the corner into the hospital section at the rear.

'Dumb really. Diamond—' he pointed to the child Iris was holding '—was playing with his pet goanna out in the back yard when Trapper—" Smitty indicated the squirming six-year-old in Dex's arms '—yeah, well, Trapper decided to not be very nice and hit Goofy with a stick.'

'Goofy?' Iris was confused.

'The goanna,' Dex said matter-of-factly.

'Oh.' Iris placed Diamond on a bed, not surprised to see Bub appearing beside them. The other patients currently in the hospital would be rather put out by the noise but Dex had been right in suggesting they bring both boys here rather than trying to deal with them in the consulting rooms.

'Goofy got mad.'

'Rightly so,' Dex agreed.

'Yeah, but Goofy upset Trapper's spider cage,' Smitty continued.

'One of them was bitten by a spider?' Iris started to check for marks on Diamond's arms. Why was Smitty being so calm and telling a yarn when his son could be dying? The little boy's mother was standing quietly to the side, her eyes wide as she looked on from a distance.

'Ah…she don't do well in hospitals,' Smitty

said, obviously following the line of Iris's gaze. 'Anyway, the spiders got onto Trapper.'

'Trapper was bitten? By what sort of spider?' Dex was looking for marks but the kid was squirming too much. 'We need to keep him still. If there's poison in his blood, moving around is the last thing we need him to do. Mate, can you lie still for me, please?'

'Nah, he didn't get bitten.'

'Then what happened?' Iris was starting to get rather impatient, wishing the father would just spit out the exact circumstances that had led them to bring their two boys here to be treated.

'Has anyone been bitten?' Dex tried, keeping his cool. He didn't blame Iris for feeling impatient. He was beginning to get there himself.

'Yes. Diamond.'

'By what?' Bub was the one who asked the question as she headed to the cabinet where the different types of antivenene were kept.

'Brown snake.'

'Where?' But even as she said the word, Iris found the two little puncture wounds on the inside of the boy's right foot. 'Found it.'

'When did all of this happen?' Dex asked.

'About ten minutes ago. We just scooped up

the boys and brought them straight here. Seemed the best thing to do.'

'And Trapper?' Dex was slowly getting the boy to calm down as he glanced over to watch Iris dealing with Diamond. At least the five-year-old wasn't thrashing about like his brother.

'The spiders crawled all over him. He doesn't like it. They're all harmless ones, none are poisonous, Doc Dex, I swear, but Trap still doesn't like the sensation.'

'I don't blame him. It's all right, mate. They're all gone.' Dex tried to soothe the six-year-old.

'I did get bitten. I did,' Trapper returned with vehemence.

'Where? Whereabouts?' Dex asked, his tone calm. 'Show me?' The sooner the boy was more in control, the sooner they'd really be able to help him.

'On the finger.' Trapper started to calm down but still kept twitching as he held out the finger in question.

'A spider bit you on the finger?' he checked, unable to see any marks.

'No. Goofy did.'

Dex relaxed a bit and took a look at the finger. 'Hmm. It looks OK to me.'

'No. It's not OK. Goofy bit me. He's naughty.'

'You was the one hittin' him with a stick,' Smitty pointed out to his son. Iris and Bub were stabilising Diamond by inserting an IV line, administering the antivenene, splinting the area and doing the required observations to ensure the boy's heart rate remained at a normal pace. The faster his blood was pumping, the faster the poison could spread around his body. Dex returned his attention back to Trapper, quite satisfied that Diamond was receiving the best care this clinic could offer in the form of their new paediatrician.

'Hey, mate. I've got a question for you.'

'What?' Trapper looked at him a little sceptically but still kept trembling.

'What happens when a goanna bites you?'

'It hurts.'

'Yep. And then what?'

'And then your whole body starts to shake and tremble.' His little brown eyes were growing wide with panic as he spoke the words. 'And then when you can't stop shaking, you know all the goanna spit is in your body and it's like all over the place and like everywhere. And then you die.' Trapper looked seriously up at Dex. 'Am I gonna die, Doc Dex?'

'Not at all.' Dex made sure his answer was

serious, even though he was hard pressed not to laugh at what Trapper had been saying. 'I do have another question, mate. Who told you about this reaction to a goanna bite?'

'Glaston.'

Dex nodded. 'Your big brother. Right.' He looked at Smitty. 'Makes sense now.'

Smitty shook his head. 'I'm gonna have a little talk with Glast when I get home. Rotten kid. He knows how his little brothers listen to everything he says.'

'No doubt he said it as a joke.' Dex kept his words quiet, not wanting to really upset Trapper or embarrass him. Thankfully, the six-year-old had stopped squirming around and was lying quite still. Dex cleaned and bandaged the boy's finger, pleased to see that Iris and Bub really did have everything under control where poor little Diamond was concerned.

'Now, Trapper,' Dex said, 'I want you to know that your finger isn't going to fall off. Everything is going to be fine. You're not sick. In fact, you're in very good health. What Glaston said was wrong.'

Iris listened with half an ear to what Dex was saying to calm the boy down. She was pleased Trapper was now settled as he'd been causing

Diamond some distress. 'Your brother's fine,' Iris told the five-year-old. 'Dr Dexter is explaining everything to Trapper and soon you'll both be up and running about the place, causing more havoc. For now, though, you've been a very lucky boy.'

She and Bub continued to treat Diamond but Iris couldn't help sneaking glances at Dex. She'd been so aware of him as they'd looked after their patients and she'd been impressed with the way he hadn't talked down to the six-year-old but instead had figured out what was wrong and then handled it well. A lot of doctors had difficulty treating children but it appeared Dex was a man of many talents.

She looked back at Diamond, focusing her thoughts on what she was doing rather than on her colleague. It was quite clear that Dex Crawford needed women to fall at his feet, to be under his thrall, and because she was resisting, he was working harder to ensure he snared her in the end.

It didn't seem to matter that she was scarred, that her body was a mass of mismatched skin and several grafts. It didn't seem to matter that she simply wasn't interested in any sort of relationship other than a purely professional one. He needed her to walk behind him with her tongue dragging on the ground, hanging on his every word. He was a playboy and, as such, he was most definitely not the type of man she was interested in.

So he was good-looking. So he had charm and charisma. So he knew how to make a girl feel special just by giving her his undivided attention. That didn't mean she had to fall at his feet. It didn't mean she would be aware of his presence even before she saw him. It wouldn't happen. She would fight it because she was strong, she was a fighter, and her life would go on long after she'd left the little outback mining town of Didja.

When Diamond was stable, Iris turned to face the boys' parents. 'I'd like Diamond to stay in overnight so we can monitor him.'

Diamond's mother was still standing in the corner and at this news she started to shake her head from side to side. Smitty went to her and placed a hand on her shoulder. 'He'll be OK. He's got Doc Dex and the new sheila to look after him. He'll be as right as rain.' Smitty looked around the room. 'And there's Bub. You trust Bub. She won't let anything happen to our Diamond.'

'No way in the world. Come along, darl,' Bub said, taking the woman by the hand. 'Let's go outside and get some fresh air and I'll explain everything. Diamond'll be apples.' Bub took Diamond's mother out of the hospital and Iris turned to face Dex.

'How's Trapper?'

'Trapper's been beaut. What a hero. Survived a goanna bite and lives to tell the tale. The kids at school are going to be rapt to hear the story on Monday.'

'And my story, too,' Diamond said weakly.

'And yours, too, mate.' Dex walked over to where Diamond lay on the hospital bed and smiled down at the boy. 'Two brave heroes in the one family. Smitty, you should be right proud of your boys.'

They continued chatting, keeping the two boys at ease, while Iris found the necessary forms and filled them in. Even though this place didn't have a lot of red tape, there were still rules and procedures to be followed, and Iris was the type of doctor who liked her *i*'s dotted and her *t*'s crossed.

Dex continued to watch her out the corner of his eye as he joked with Smitty and the boys. He knew he'd been lying to himself about only wanting to have a professional friendship with Iris. The woman was enchanting.

He wanted to know more about her, wanted to

talk to her, to find out about her past, about her scars, to help her in any way he could. He was having difficulty controlling his thoughts where she was concerned. A woman, so vibrant, so beautiful, and yet when he'd looked deeply into her eyes before he'd left last night, he'd seen the tortured soul beneath the exterior.

He wanted to know her, to be able to look at her scars, to touch them, to kiss them. He wanted to pull her hair from the plait, to see how it looked floating about her face, her shoulders, down her back. He wanted to caress the smattering of freckles across her nose and he wanted the opportunity to really taste those lips.

Never before had a woman consumed his thoughts as much as Iris. She'd been married. She'd lost her husband and that would have changed her. He wondered what she'd been like before her tragedy. Whether she'd viewed the world through rose-coloured glasses or if she'd been as closed off then as she was now.

Dex also knew he was moving into uncharted territory as far as women were concerned. He'd always held himself aloof, friends with everyone, serious with no one. Yet the way he was constantly thinking about Iris had come completely out of left field and he wasn't quite sure what to do about it. However, the need, the intensity of the way he thought about her, it was there and he couldn't deny the attraction, the gravitational pull towards his new colleague.

It didn't even matter that she appeared to want to have nothing to do with him, except in a professional capacity. She'd opened up to him, shared a part of herself with him, had sobbed in his arms and allowed him to comfort her. She'd touched a part of him deep down in his soul that he'd kept hidden from everyone, especially during the past couple of years when he'd been so estranged from his adoptive family.

In fact, being with Iris last night, supporting her, being there for her, had made Dex think about his siblings. He'd been so hurt, so angry when he'd found out he was adopted that he'd just cut himself off from all of them. It hadn't been Alexandria's and Mason's fault and he wouldn't blame them if they never spoke to him again… although he hoped they would. Having Melissa in his life had made him miss the twins even more than before. They'd grown up with him as their older brother. They hadn't known the truth either and he knew they weren't to blame.

His parents, however… No. It was too soon to think about his parents. They'd lied to him and that was something he just couldn't forgive. Not yet, at any rate.

Looking back at Trapper and Diamond and the way they interacted, the younger of the two drowsing due to the sedative Iris had administered whilst his brother recounted again—with actions—how Goofy had bitten his finger, Dex still wasn't sure where the snake had come into it but given there were quite a few brown snakes around in the outback, and knowing that Smitty's back yard was wildly overgrown, he could sort of see how in the mix of goannas, spider cages and two boys playing outside, Diamond could have been bitten by a snake. They were brothers. Brothers who had just been being brothers. Having fun. Being naughty. Making mischief.

Dex exhaled harshly as he admitted to himself that he missed Mason and he missed Alexandria. Joss was like a brother to him but that was also more of an equal type of relationship. With the twins, he was their big brother. He always had been and he always would be. The pain within his heart, the pain at accepting the fact that he truly missed them, started to become overwhelming.

He felt as though the walls were closing in on him. He needed time. He needed space. He needed a rocket ship to get him out of here.

'Are you all right, Dex?' Iris looked at him, a little concerned.

'Huh?' He hadn't realised she was standing near him. He looked down at the papers she held out to him, not really seeing them. His thoughts came jolting back to the present with a thud. He looked around the room, at Smitty and his boys. Then he looked at Iris. The beautiful, emotionally traumatised Iris who was being so brave. She'd been through such turmoil and yet she stood strong and sure, getting on with her life, moving forward.

His world had come crumbling down around him, though not in such a violent way as Iris had experienced, and what had he done? He'd left. He'd told his family to leave him alone, then he'd wrapped his car around a tree. If it hadn't been for Joss offering him the job in Didja… Dex shook his head, not wanting to think about what might have happened. He'd been in a bad place back then and since arriving in the outback town he'd shut himself off to all deep and meaningful relationships.

Now, though, there was Iris. Making him feel.

Making him want to know more about her. He wanted to spend time just talking to her, being with her, helping her. She made him *want* to invest his time, his effort in really helping. It was so strange because he'd never felt such a strong desire like this before. Oh, sure, he helped his patients. He chatted with people at the pub. He dated women, but none of that provided a lasting connection, a blending of hearts, minds and souls. Yet with Iris…

'Dex?' She said his name again and this time there was a slight hint of concern in her voice.

Dex shook his head. 'Sorry.' He took the proffered papers. 'You need me to sign these? Sure.' He scribbled his signature where it needed to be and handed the papers back to Iris. 'Well…now that the crisis has been averted, I might head off.' Dex jerked his thumb at the door. Too many thoughts. Too many emotions. Too many desires to fight when all he wanted to do was to release her hair from its bonds and then run his fingers through her glorious locks.

This wasn't right. The way she was making him feel was everything he'd vowed never to enter into again.

Iris watched him withdraw, almost stumbling

over his own feet as he walked backwards towards the door. What was wrong? Had *she* done something wrong? Had he not wanted to get the paperwork out of the way? All of a sudden he seemed as jittery as a long-tailed cat in a room full of rocking chairs, wanting to be anywhere else but here. She tried to think back. Had she said something to upset him? Had she annoyed him in some way?

Whilst she wasn't interested in him in a romantic way at all, it didn't mean she wanted to offend him in a professional capacity. They would be required to work together for the next six months and it would be best for everyone concerned if that was a happy relationship. Still, the fact remained. Dex wasn't behaving at all like the Dex she'd known over the past week.

'You don't need me any more, do you, Iris?'

She raised her eyebrows at his question. What? He wasn't going to reiterate his dinner invitation? He wasn't going to try and cajole her into going out with him to Stiggie's tonight? Wasn't going to turn on the charm? 'Er…no.'

'OK. Have a good rest of the day.' He waved to their patients. 'See you around, Smitty. Take care, boys.' With that, he was gone. Out of the doors and far away.

It was probably just as well, Iris thought as she put the signed papers back on Bub's desk at the nurses' station. Having Dex around made her mind go funny, and when he wasn't near her she could think more clearly. Get more done.

'Yeah,' she whispered softly to herself. 'You're not affected by him at all.' She shook her head. 'Liar.'

CHAPTER SIX

THROUGHOUT the following week, Iris did her level best to be professional where her dealings with Dexter were concerned. Keeping her distance wasn't too difficult, although there were a few occasions where they were required to work side by side.

Iris had to admit that he really was good at what he did. His mind moved like lightning and his bedside manner with all his patients was perfect. He kept them relaxed and at ease, even in some terrible situations.

On Wednesday, Areva knocked on her consulting room door, alerting Iris to the fact that Dex needed her in the hospital emergency room.

'Hope Bundabirra was brought in by her parents with a large stick in her abdomen,' Areva said as they walked quickly towards the hospital section of the clinic.

Iris fired off questions. 'How old is she?' The

more information she had, the better she'd be able to treat Hope.

'Thirteen.'

'Siblings?'

'Two younger brothers.'

'And the stick is *in* her abdomen? Impaled?'

'I'm not sure. Juanita—uh, she's the nurse who's rostered on today for any emergencies— just gave me the basic details when Dex told her to call through for you.'

'Do you know if Hope has any allergies?'

'I don't know about medicines but she is allergic to shellfish. Does that help?'

Iris paused at the door to the hospital and smiled at Areva. 'It does. Thanks.' Iris left the receptionist and headed through to the emergency room.

'Hi, there,' Dex greeted her cheerfully, his smile playing havoc with her senses. She wished he wouldn't. Iris pulled herself together and forced a polite smile, more for the patient's sake than for her colleagues.

'What's up?'

'Ta-dah!' Dex waved his hands magically and pointed to Hope's abdomen. Iris tried not to blink too hard at what she saw. A stick, about one centimetre in diameter, was protruding out of Hope's left side, near her hip. There was dried blood around the wound site and the girl's white top, which wasn't that white any more, had been cut to allow greater access to the area.

'Wow. Impressive.' She smiled at the teenager. 'Hi, Hope. I'm Iris.'

'Hey.'

'How did this happen?' Iris continued to look the girl over, noting red patches where bruises would later form on her arms, legs and face. There were also several scratches and quite a lot of grazing, especially around the heels of her hands.

'I've already told Doc Dex,' she said, her tone a little sullen.

'You answer the doctor, Hope,' her mother said sternly, and the teenager rolled her eyes.

'Fine. I was running home from school with my friend Nancy and I tripped.'

'That's it?'

'I fell.'

'And the stick just went into your abdomen?'

'I fell at a strange angle.'

Iris glanced quickly at Dex and could see that he wasn't buying the story either. At the moment, though, the real reason why Hope hadn't told the truth didn't matter. They needed to treat her wound and stabilise her. 'You seem very calm about it all.'

Hope shrugged. 'No sense in fussing.'

'She had some paracetamol when she came home,' her mother announced. 'I cleaned her up as best I could but when I saw that thing sticking out of her belly…' Hope's mother shuddered.

'You were right to bring her straight here,' Dex said placatingly. 'However, if you'd like to wait outside, we'll get to work with removing the obstruction. Go and chat with Bub. I'm sure she'd love to see you.'

Hope's mother nodded before leaving Dex, Iris and Juanita to care for her daughter.

'I've already set up an IV and started antibiotics,' Dex told Iris as he handed her the patient's medical notes. Iris read quickly, noting no allergies, except the shellfish Areva had already mentioned.

'Are you going to, like, knock me out?' Hope asked.

Iris smiled and nodded. 'It'll be easier for you to have a general anaesthetic.'

'You won't feel a thing,' Dex told the girl. Juanita continued to prepare the instruments the two doctors would require for removal and debridement of the wound. Iris walked over to the sink to wash her hands and to pull on gloves. She *felt* rather than heard Dex approach, and warmth from his body as he stood quite close to her was enough to make her skin break out in excited goose bumps.

'Ever done anything like this before?' he asked, standing beside her and washing his own hands, whilst Juanita continued to monitor Hope.

'A few times.'

'Good.'

Iris glanced at him. 'You don't believe her story, do you? About what happened?'

Dex scoffed and rolled his eyes. 'Not likely,' he said quietly. 'Don't push it with her. She'll tell us before too long.'

'How do you know? Dex, something the size of that stick doesn't get lodged in a person's body because they "tripped" over.'

Dex edged a little closer and spoke in a conspiratorial whisper, the earthly scent she equated with him settling over her delightfully. 'I know that. You know that, but Hope doesn't know that we know. You know?'

Iris couldn't help the laugh that bubbled out of her. She turned, wiping her hands dry before pulling on a sterile gown to protect her clothes and a pair of gloves, needing some sort of distance between herself and Dex. He was fun. She had to give him that. The only problem was, it only made it more difficult to keep her distance from him.

'Right, Hope. How are you feeling?' Dex walked back to their patient's bedside, ready to get the proceedings under way.

'Drowsy.' Her words were spoken slowly and Dex did a skin-prick test on the area around the protruding stick.

'Feel anything?'

'Feel just fine,' she drawled, lying back on the pillows, before succumbing to the anaesthetic.

'I'd say we're ready.' Dex nodded to Iris.

Dex monitored Hope, whilst marvelling at Iris's clever and stable fingers, never wavering, always sure of the next move. That was how he was with women, wasn't it? Always sure of the next move? Yet with Iris that didn't seem to be the case. Was that what he was doing at the moment? Planning his next move? Or was the distance he'd also been attempting to maintain between them part of that next move? Was his next move to ensure he stayed as far away from her as possible?

Too many questions.

When Iris finally managed to remove the stick,

Juanita was at the ready with gauze to pack the wound the instant the obstruction was removed. They debrided the area and had a good look around.

'She's been very lucky,' Iris said softly. 'No major organ damage. She'll be fine.' Dex reversed the anaesthetic and together they monitored Hope's recovery.

'How are you feeling?' Dex asked.

'Fine, fine, fine.' The words were mumbled one over the other as she started to regain proper consciousness. Hope was lying back on the white pillows, her dark hair and skin stark in contrast.

'You don't need to protect whoever did this to you.'

'Yep. I do.'

'No.' Dex was adamant. He looked at Iris, almost as though he was silently seeking some sort of approval. Iris nodded, encouraging him on in whatever he had in mind. If he had some sort of hunch as to what had really happened to their patient, he needed to play those cards in order for the truth to come out.

'You know…' His voice was calm, as smooth as silk, reassuring. Iris liked hearing those deep tones of his. So soothing. 'Nancy's brother has been in trouble with the law before and if you don't say anything, he's going to think he can do to other people what he's done to you.'

'But Nancy. He'll hurt Nancy.' Hope closed her eyes and shook her head.

'We can protect Nancy. We can protect you, Hope. You need to speak up about this.'

Iris looked at the girl, who was wavering on the edge of sleep, seeing worried lines mar her brow, and her heart went out to the child. She was only thirteen and yet her life didn't seem at all simple right now.

'She's asleep,' Juanita announced.

'Monitor her,' he said as he headed for the door.

'Where are you going?' Juanita asked, but Dex didn't reply.

'He's going to call the police,' Iris answered, knowing he was a man who not only cared about his patient but cared far too intensely about this entire community. Despite what she thought of him, despite the attraction she felt for him, there was one thing she knew for certain. Dex Crawford was a good man and they were definitely hard to find.

Two and a half weeks after the emergency with Hope, Iris went into her apartment and sank down on the lounge, pulling her hair from its plaited bond. Hope had stayed in hospital for over a week, Bub and Dex coaxing the teenager to own up to the truth. Finally Hope had been brave and done the right thing, pressing charges against Nancy's older brother.

Iris had taken to counselling both girls on a regular basis as a social worker only came to Didja once a month. It was something that had drawn her right into the heart of the community. She'd assisted with Nancy being temporarily taken from her home where her apathetic father couldn't care less about her, and had placed her with her aunt, who'd been trying to get guardianship of the teenager for quite some time.

'What a day!' Iris had now been in Didja for a whole month and she doubted she'd ever get used to the heat, the constant need to swat flies and the overly chatty patients. Not that she minded. She liked people. She'd always classified herself as a people person but today, for some reason, everyone who'd come to see her in the clinic had wanted to tell her their life stories, and in return they had wanted to know hers.

She'd had to field questions and speculations and to top it all off, she'd ended up finishing far later than she would have liked. Joss and Melissa had been away all day, doing house calls, which had left a busier clinic than usual for herself and Dex.

Iris closed her eyes and rested her head back on a cushion. Dexter Crawford. The man was an enigma and one she'd been trying to stop thinking about for the past month. He was definitely turning out to be…more than she'd bargained for.

Ever since that Saturday when little Diamond and Trapper had presented for treatment, Dex had been different. Throughout her first week in Didja Dex had been the playboy she'd pegged him for. She'd noticed the way other women looked at him and she'd watched as he'd charmed them all. He also seemed to hold himself so apart from them that she couldn't help but wonder whether he'd been burned in love in the past.

He hadn't, however, held himself aloof on the night she'd broken down. Iris shook her head at the memory, embarrassment still tingeing her cheeks. She'd cried and he'd held her. The memory was a difficult one to wipe away, especially when she remembered the sensation of being encircled within his strong, firm arms. She'd felt so…protected and she hadn't felt that way in a very long time. He'd also made her feel precious, as though she really was important to him, to Didja, to the world.

Too many times in those first few years after Tim's death Iris had wished she'd died too. Yet for the first time, whilst she'd been in Dex's arms, she'd honestly started to believe that she still had a lot to offer this great big world, and it was because of him that she'd felt that way.

Then Dex had touched her back. He'd felt the scars. He'd guessed she'd been a victim of a fire, that she was scarred in more places than just her back. He'd been repulsed and for the past few weeks he'd maintained a professional distance. Iris eyes closed tighter as she tried to ignore the pain of Dex's rejection. She didn't blame him, she knew her body wasn't something any man wanted to look at, let alone touch.

Dex, like every other red-blooded male on the planet, liked women who were gorgeous, who were complete—not freaks. She didn't want to be so attracted to him and she was pleased he'd stayed as far away from her as she had from him. The more distance they could maintain, the easier it would be to continue with her work here in the Didja community.

Still the thoughts twirled around and around in

her head. Dex didn't want her. No man wanted her. Focusing on her work was all she was good for. Dex hadn't really meant to offer such heart-warming compassion that night. He'd no doubt been trying to keep his distance but then she'd burst into tears and he'd felt compelled to comfort her. She wasn't attractive. She was scarred and as her breathing started to increase, she rocked slowly back and forth.

Tears started to bite at the back of her eyes but it was too late. Her mind had gone to the place she never usually allowed it to go. 'No.' The word was an agonised whisper as she started to feel, to smell, to panic.

The flames. The heat. The terror. She'd woken. Sat up with a start, instinct telling her something was wrong. She'd immediately reached out to shake Tim, to wake him up.

'Tim. Tim!'

'What? Did the hospital call?'

She'd always marvelled that for an obstetrician who was used to delivering babies at all hours, Tim was able to sleep so deeply and sometimes didn't hear the phone ring unless it was right beside his ear.

'Something's wrong.' She'd listened carefully

and then she'd breathed in deeply. 'Smoke! Tim. I can smell smoke.'

He'd turned over, still half-groggy. 'Why are you whispering? If the house is on fire, whispering isn't going to make it go away.' He'd grinned at her, that stupid silly grin that had made her fall in love with him in the first place.

'Tim!' The seriousness in her voice had stopped him from teasing and he'd sat up, sniffing the air. Then his eyes had widened and he'd sat up straighter. He'd breathed deeper.

'I do smell smoke. It's very acrid.' He cautiously climbed from the bed and walked to their bedroom door. Iris swallowed over the lump in her throat as she watched him, her hands clenched tightly around the bedsheets. She was usually a woman of action, a woman who liked to take charge, to be in control, but at that moment she was gripped with such overpowering terror and fear that movement was impossible.

'Be careful.' The words had no sound as they came from her lips but when he opened the door and padded into the hallway, she heard him start to cough. A moment later the smoke alarms started blaring, beeping their warning signal. It was enough of a shock to break her from her trance and Iris sprang out of bed, pulled on the first set of clothes she found and started shoving as much as she could into a bag.

Clothes. Jewellery. Photographs. Trinkets. Things. Useless things she'd realised much later as she'd woken up in hospital, lying on her stomach in the burns unit. The fire had well and truly taken hold at the rear of their house, which had backed onto a national park. Of course, Tim, being the big damn hero that he was, had decided to fight the fire, to put it out, to save their home.

Iris turned her head from side to side, her hair knotting and sliding around her face, the tears breaking over her in one wave after the other. 'No. No! Why didn't you listen?'

She'd screamed for him to come back. She'd shoved the bag of things out of the front bedroom window and gone to get her husband. They'd needed to get out of the house. Nothing else had mattered but their lives. Everything could be replaced…everything except human life.

'Stupid. Why? *Why?*' she whispered, anger at his idiocy coursing through her.

She sat upright, her vision completely blurred by the tears sliding down her cheeks as she cried. Grabbing the nearest object she could find, she picked it up and hurled it against the wall with mounting fury.

The loud sound pierced her reverie and it took a split second for her to realise what she'd done. She'd smashed a vase. An empty vase, which had been provided with the rest of the furnishings. A vase that didn't belong to her. Wiping at her eyes and swallowing over the lumps in her throat, she scrambled across the floor and started to pick up the pieces, illogically trying to fit them back together again. When her trembling fingers couldn't make them stick, a fresh wave of tears erupted and she crouched in the corner, her anger, her frustration, her pain seeping from her as it never had before.

'Iris?'

'I don't want this,' she whimpered, her face almost covered over with her wild hair.

'Iris. It's me. Dex.'

'I don't want this,' she said again, her words more forceful. She was still in the corner, her arms wrapped around her knees as she slowly lifted her head to look blindly at the man before her.

'Dex?' Her tone was almost confused at finding him there.

'Shh.' Dex bent down and sat on the floor near

her, mindful of the broken glass. So *that's* what had shattered against the wall, startling him beyond belief. He'd stopped making his dinner, ensuring everything was switched off, before heading next door. The door had been locked but thankfully he had a master key. As an owner of the clinic, it was a security measure both he and Joss employed, although this was the first time he'd ever used the key.

'I hate it.' Iris's tone was full of fear.

'I know.'

Dex didn't make any attempt to touch her. No, of course he wouldn't. She was the elephant queen. She was scarred, she was broken. What man in their right mind would ever want her?

'Iris. What is it?' Dex could hardly see her face through her mass of hair, hair his fingers itched to touch, to smooth away from her face, but now was not the time. She needed him and he'd be here for her. The feeling that he could help, that he could really do something for her, filled him with a warmth he hadn't felt in a very long time. Perhaps because he'd been so self-centred, so self-focused as he'd tried to heal his own hurts, he'd forgotten just how good it felt to help someone else.

He waited a while for her to answer but she

kept staring out into nothingness, hiccuping now and then as the tears dried on her cheeks. He looked around the room and spotted a box of tissues on the coffee table. He leaned over for them, reaching with his hand and only just managing to grab them. He placed them on the floor next to her. She didn't seem to notice.

'Iris?' He tried again and this time put a hand on her arm. Her gaze flicked up to glare at him as she flinched. Dex immediately withdrew his hand. 'Sorry. I just want to help.' He shrugged. 'I'm not sure how, though.' The last he muttered more to himself than to her.

Iris looked away and Dex was once again left trying to decide what to do. Should he leave? No. She was in a far worse state than she'd been the last time he'd seen her like this. Perhaps he should give her some space. Go and put the kettle on, or see if she had anything stronger than tea. Whisky. Brandy. If she didn't have any, he could run down to the pub and get some. Whatever she needed, he'd be there to help with.

'Idiot.'

Dex looked at Iris. 'All right. Not what I was going for. Hero. Gallant knight. Rescuer even. I'd have settled for any one of those.'

Iris closed her eyes, feeling a lot of the tension leave her at his words. This time when she opened her eyes to look at him, she was really looking at him, able to focus on the present, not the past.

'I didn't mean you.'

'Oh, well, that's pleasing to know.' He withdrew a tissue from the box and held it out to her. She took it. 'I hope that means I'm still in with a chance for one of my options, then.'

Iris couldn't help the smile that tugged at her lips, although it was a rather tired one. 'I wouldn't want your ego to swell.' She accepted the tissue and dabbed at her eyes.

Dex chuckled. 'Fair enough.'

'I must look a sight.'

'No. You look…' Unable to stop himself, he reached out and brushed her hair from her face, the soft silky strands smooth and glorious as he tucked them behind her ears. He brushed a thumb over the smattering of freckles that kissed her nose and cheeks. 'Lovely.'

'Liar.'

He nodded at that, realising she was incapable of accepting his truth. 'Possibly, but it's been my experience to tell the occasional white lie, especially when a woman has been crying.'

'Experience.' She breathed in, her breath catching as she recovered from crying. 'You've had plenty of that.'

'I meant my sister.'

'Melissa?' Total confusion reigned through her clouded mind. 'When was she ups—?'

'Not Melissa. My other sister.'

Iris stopped at that, sort of pleased he wasn't pushing her to talk about her past. She felt foolish enough that he'd come in to witness her break-down. 'What's her name?'

'Xandi. Alexandria is her full name.' He almost sighed as he spoke.

'You miss her?'

'I do, and Mason too. They're twins.'

'How much younger?' Iris knew a bit about Dex but it was more of the background as to why he'd been adopted in the first place, rather than the actual life he'd led.

'Almost seven years.' He shook his head. 'So many clues. They were all there. You think I would have twigged.'

'Meaning?'

'I remember my mother going to the doctor's a lot. Of course, most of her appointments were whilst I was at school but now I know she'd been going to an in vitro fertilisation clinic. It's how she became pregnant with the twins. It's why we're so far apart in age. It's why we don't look anything like each other. Xandi's almost the spitting image of my mother and Mason, well, let's just say the apple doesn't fall far from the tree. I just can't believe I didn't see it.'

'You're still hurting.' It was a statement as the tone of his voice had become quite dark and vehement.

'I was stupid.'

'You weren't stupid, Dex.'

'No. I was an idiot. You were right before.'

'I didn't call *you* an idiot,' she pointed out.

'Who did you call an idiot?' His sudden change of subject surprised her. 'Who was it who made you throw that vase? Who made you cry so badly, it looks as though your heart's been broken all over again?' Dex was pretty sure he knew the answer but he guessed Iris had a few things of her own she hadn't faced.

They were a pair. Both of them running from their pasts. He'd needed to turn the conversation back onto her to get the focus off himself. Thinking about his siblings only made him angry and he didn't want to be angry right now. He wanted to be supportive.

Apart from that, he wanted to know about her past, her tragedy…the fire. The woman had not only been plaguing his dreams but his daytime thoughts as well. More often than not, he found himself wondering what exactly had happened to her. Why had she decided to come to Didja? Why now? He also wanted to discover if there was anything specific that was triggering these outbursts of hers. If so, why were they coming now? From what she'd said before, it had been quite a few years since her husband had died. Why were old memories, thoughts, events surfacing now? What had happened to trigger it all again?

Or perhaps, it wasn't 'again'. Perhaps Iris had locked her thoughts, her inner most feelings away so deeply that they were only now beginning to surface. She'd left Sydney, she'd stepped outside of her comfort zone and perhaps that was all the catalyst she'd needed to get her through to the next stage in her grieving process.

'If it wasn't me,' he pushed again, 'then who? Who are you so mad at?'

'My husband. Tim.' Her words were flat, deflated, and yet the pain was still there.

'He died in the fire?' It was the best guess and one his gut instinct told him was spot on.

'Yes.' Iris looked past him, her words soft and matter-of-fact. 'I called to him. I told him to come back. To get out. But he wouldn't listen.'

She was back there. Back in the smoke-filled corridor of her house, running in slow motion to where Tim was in the kitchen.

'He was filling buckets of water and tossing them onto the flames that were licking at the doorway from the back of the house. The heat was intense. The smoke was rolling on the ceiling. The fire alarms were beeping. I grabbed his arm. I tried to pull him from the room. He wanted to fight the stupid fire. Idiot.'

'You're angry with him.'

Iris blinked and looked over at Dex, only then realising she'd been speaking out loud. 'Yes. The house was irrelevant. Everything was irrelevant. Nothing mattered. In that one instant nothing mattered. Not the house or the things in it. Not the cars, not the status in the neighbourhood or at work. Nothing mattered more than our lives and Tim…he just didn't seem to realise that. He kept saying it wasn't too bad. That he could put the fire out. He told me to go. Told me to ring the neighbours. To warn them. To call the fire brigade. He was in management mode. He was in charge and you didn't argue with Tim when he was in charge.' There was angry humour in her words.

'Except he wasn't,' Dex guessed.

'No. The fire was.' Iris raised a hand to cover her eyes as a fresh bout of tears loomed. 'He was an idiot.'

'He was acting on instinct.'

Iris dropped her hand and glared at him. 'Then his instincts were wrong.'

'Yes. They were. He made a mistake. He paid the ultimate price. It's tragic but you lived, Iris. You survived.'

'I went back for him.' She shook her head. 'It was wrong but I couldn't…I just couldn't.' The tears came again and she didn't try to stop them. She needed to talk. She needed to say these words out loud, words she hadn't spoken to anyone—ever.

'He was lying there. A beam had fallen.' She swallowed. 'It didn't matter. It had knocked him unconscious so he didn't feel a thing. I tried to get him out. I grabbed his arms and I pulled. I probably severed his spinal c—' She stopped and looked at Dex. 'The heat was so intense. The smoke filled my lungs, stung at my eyes. It was trying to choke me. I fell down, still tugging at Tim's hands, silently begging him to get out. He didn't. He left me. He loved the status, the house, the cars, the…the *everything* more than he loved me. He left me!'

'I doubt it was a conscious decision, Iris. He was just trying to protect his home.'

'Why didn't he try to protect *me*?' The words were spoken quietly. 'Why didn't he choose to come with *me*? To stay with *me*? To listen to *me*?'

'I don't know, but he didn't and you need to accept that. He's gone.' Dex placed a hand on her cheek, cupping the smooth skin. The fire hadn't touched her face. There were no scars there, not that he cared. He knew some people thought him shallow, that he went from one woman to the next because he was too afraid of commitment, but it wasn't shallowness that kept him from seeking out a permanent relationship.

It was the fear of getting hurt. Pure and simple.

No, he didn't care about Iris's scars. She was incredibly beautiful and he was sure she had no idea of that fact. He hoped she'd let him show her, let her see how she was perceived through another person's eyes. He was also pleased with the fact that she wasn't shrinking away from his touch.

'I hate him for leaving me.'

'And you have every right to feel that way.'

Iris looked at him then. Her big green eyes were filled with uncertainty. 'Really?'

'Yes. Iris, your emotions are your own. No one can tell you what to do, what to think, or what's right or wrong. If you feel a certain way, then *feel* it. Be angry at him. Hate him for leaving you, because once you acknowledge the emotion, only then can you start to heal.' After he'd spoken these words, he slowly dropped his hand. It was as though he was also talking to himself.

'Wow.'

'What?'

'I don't know. You continually surprise me, Dex Crawford.' Iris shook her head, pulled out another tissue and blew her nose. 'How do you know so much? You did a minor in psychology?'

'No.' He shook his head and started to carefully gather up the pieces of broken vase. 'The way you feel about your husband is how I feel about my parents.'

'Because they lied to you?'

'Yes.'

'So you've been owning your emotions?' There was a hint of scepticism in her words.

He laughed without humour. 'Only within the last few weeks. It's as though something's changed, something's happened in my life, and things are…well, they're different.'

'Is it Melissa?'

'No.' He shook his head. 'Whatever it is, it has me thinking about my brother and sister again. It has me wondering what my parents are doing.'

'You want to see them again?'

'I don't know if I'd go that far just yet, but the fact that I'm thinking about it…'

'Acknowledging your emotions.' Iris nodded slowly as she pushed her hair back from her face.

'Exactly.' He stood and carried the broken fragments to the bin in the kitchen. Was that what his life was like? Broken fragments? If so, how on earth was he supposed to piece it back together?

When he returned, Iris was starting to stand up. She wobbled, her leg having fallen asleep in the cramped position, and Dex's arms instantly came around her.

'You all right?' he asked, his breath fanning across her face, wisps of her strawberry-blonde hair rising slightly. Gosh, she smelled good. Did she have any idea just how insane she made him feel?

'I'm fine. Thanks.' She leaned into him, feeling highly self-conscious as his hands touched her back. It felt so good to be touched. Did he have any idea of just how good he felt? Iris closed her eyes for a second, savouring the moment of being in his arms once more. She half expected him to let go because what man in his right mind would want her? She was defective.

She shifted and put weight on her leg then winced with the sparkling pain.

'Pins and needles?' he asked, and she eased back a little, opening her eyes so she could look at him. They were close. Their breath mingling together as the atmosphere around them grew tense with intimacy.

'Uhuh.' Iris swallowed over the sudden dryness in her throat. Dex was looking down at her, his brown eyes intense and powerful. His gaze dropped to her mouth and her lips parted at the same time her heart rate increased. 'Dex.' His name was a whisper upon her lips.

'Iris.' He shook his head very slowly from side to side. 'Forgive me.'

She'd been about to ask for what when he quickly lowered his head, claiming her lips with his own.

The kiss was real. This wasn't her dreaming. Dex's lips were on hers. Iris wasn't sure whether to wrap her arms about his neck, urging him to deepen the kiss, or to pull back, putting distance between them and therefore denying what she really wanted.

He'd tried to sneak a kiss once before, wanting to press his lips to hers without her consent, on that very first day they'd met. If he'd had any idea back then just how much Iris Tennant was going to plague his thoughts, he might not have attempted such a crazy stunt. Ever since that moment, he'd been working his way back here, even though he hadn't realised it until now.

He wanted to kiss her. He'd dreamed about kissing her, about holding her as he was now, about being close, about having the opportunity to taste her. He'd known she'd be gorgeous, her mouth sweeter than any he'd ever kissed before, her lips plump and ripe and, oh, so ready for him. Yet the last time he'd dared to be this close to her, she'd recoiled and slapped him across the face. Dex stilled, unsure what was about to come, waiting to see what she'd do. Was he about to be rejected again?

When she leaned into him, the pressure, oh, so slight and imperceptible, when she shifted her weight to bring their bodies a millimetre closer, when she sighed with utter longing—only then, when he felt her acceptance of what was happening, did he allow himself to move.

She wanted him and he wanted her. Their lives were about to change and both of them knew it.

CHAPTER SEVEN

DEX couldn't believe she was accepting him.

Iris was accepting his advances and something in his heart tightened with delight. He had no idea what was happening between them and he'd never felt this way before.

Her mouth was a perfect fit to his own and he closed his eyes, concentrating on holding her close but not too close, keeping the kiss intense but not too intense, making sure she kept up with him every step of the way. He didn't want to do anything to frighten her, to make her pull away. Nice and easy. That's what was required with someone as special as Iris.

The warmth between them increased as his mouth moved over hers, his tongue slipping between her lips. The movements were slow, steady and incredibly seductive. She knew he'd kissed many women before but she didn't want to think about that now. She didn't want to think about the scars on her body, or the fact that he was her colleague. She didn't want to think about anything other than the way Dex was currently making her feel.

The past, the present and the future were all wiped out. At this moment in time it was only the two of them who existed. The two of them who were caught up with such a powerful need. One on one. Each giving, each receiving. She didn't want to think about the consequences, the 'what-ifs' that would undoubtedly come later. She wanted to think about the way she seemed to be as attuned to him as he was to her, about how his body felt beneath her touch.

One hand was on his shoulder for support, the other was pressed to his chest. She opened her fingers, splaying them wide as she allowed her fingers the pleasure of feeling his firm, muscled torso. The cotton of his open-necked shirt was rough and a little coarse but as she moved a little lower, towards the buttons, she knew all of that would be changing soon enough.

She undid one, then two buttons, and it was enough for her to slide her hand underneath, her breath catching as she touched her fingers to his skin. Dex moaned and eased his body back just slightly to allow her more access to him. Iris couldn't have been happier to realise she affected him. His mouth ravaged her senses, keeping the pressure light yet slow, and she trembled with mounting anticipation.

His chest was smooth, covered with a smattering of hair that only made her fingertips tingle even more as she rubbed back and forth, loving the warmth of skin against skin. It had been so incredibly long since she'd touched a man, so long since she'd been kissed as if she was a desirable woman. Dex had the ability to make her forget everything and she was grateful for that.

Being lost in Dex meant she didn't have to face any of the plaguing emotions that often left her crying herself to sleep. There was only the two of them, nothing else. The feel, the heat, the touch, the passion. All of them were growing in intensity and she didn't want it to stop.

'Iris.' He whispered her name against her lips but she wasn't having any of it. Sliding her hand up the expanse of his chest to his neck, she cupped his cheek, her other hand urging his head to stay exactly where it was. She didn't want to talk. She wanted to feel. She hadn't felt so much in so long and she didn't want it to end.

The scent of him, the feel of him, the taste of him—all of it was an intoxicating cocktail and much more potent than any bartender could mix. This was Dex and he was kissing her, kissing her as though she were a desirable, beautiful and intelligent woman. Kissing her as though she were the type of woman he usually kissed. Kissing her as though he really meant it.

Right at this moment, as his mouth continued to create sweet torture with hers, his slow and sensual approach winning her over with each passing second, she didn't care if he was only kissing her because he wanted to know what it was like to kiss a freak. To kiss a woman who was scarred, who had physical reminders of a past trauma.

His mouth was still moving against hers in such perfect synchronicity she was sure she was about to melt at his feet. Fireworks were exploding within her, tingles were spreading through her body, especially when he shifted to press his chest firmly against her own.

On and on the desire raged and Iris couldn't believe how magnificent he was. She knew these kisses they were sharing probably didn't mean as much to him as they did to her and in that split second a ridiculous competitive urge kicked in and she found herself deepening the kiss, wanting to take him higher.

The pressure increased, the intensity was more powerful than before, and the passion burst forth as hunger met hunger. To say he was surprised was an understatement. He'd wanted to let Iris know he wasn't about to take advantage of her. He'd wanted to kiss her, so he had and he'd decided to keep everything light and simple, slow and sensual but this…this deep-seated passion she was sharing with him made the blood pump faster around his body.

Her hands were at the base of his neck, fingers splayed out into his hair, ensuring his head stayed exactly where it was. Her mouth was full of heat and need. The pressure was hard and firm. She was dynamic and he matched her frantic kisses stroke for stroke. They were both in this. They were both feeling the same tumultuous emotions. They both wanted this badly.

Never before had he allowed his need for a woman to drive him over the edge, but Iris was something different. She definitely wasn't like the other women he'd dated, she was better. She was not only highly intelligent and as sexy as all get-out but she was on the same wavelength as him. She'd been hurt, she'd experienced betrayal and anguish, and whilst their circumstances had been completely different, the emotions were incredibly similar. She understood him without him needing to explain it in fancy terms.

She was wild. Evocative. Delightful…vulnerable.

The silky strands of her long hair sifted through his fingers as, unable to stop himself, he gathered her closer still, running his hands down her back. The scars were there. He could feel them through her long-sleeved cotton shirt and he wanted to see them, to kiss them, to tenderly run his finger along them. They were a part of her natural beauty and he accepted that.

He slid his hands lower, down to where her untucked shirt hung around her derrière. The need to touch her, to feel his hands on her skin as she had done with him, was becoming overwhelming. The heat, the fusion, the power. It was raw and bordering on wild, and the need for touch was too much to deny.

The heat was starting to become unbearable yet he craved it more than anything. She was delicious, attentive and hungry for more. He met that hunger, wanting to provide what she needed and at the same time take what he wanted.

He broke his mouth free from hers but only to place electrifying kisses on her face, her ear and down her neck. Iris sucked in air as she tilted her head back, allowing him the access he sought. The power surging through them both was equally matched and she held on to those broad, firm shoulders of his, not wanting him to go anywhere.

'Iris.' Her name was a husky caress on his lips as he nudged the collar of her shirt aside. He wanted her badly and he needed her to want him just as much.

His name was on her trembling, parted lips. How had he been able to make her lose control, to make her want and to feel as she hadn't in such a very long time? It was glorious to feel this way, to have his lips creating such havoc with her equilibrium. Her breathing was erratic, her body was a mass of tingles and he was kissing her. Nothing mattered. Just the feel. Just the want. Just the need that both of them shared.

His mouth slid lower at her neck, his hands slid higher at her back, the touch of his hands on her caused a powerful heat to suffuse her entire body…a powerful heat that was followed by a thousand alarm bells.

Her scars!

Iris's eyes snapped open. His fingers were nanoseconds away from touching the scars on the bared skin of her back. Instant panic replaced the heat and passion that had enthralled her. Her breathing was still erratic but this time it was from fear rather than desire.

'No,' she whispered. 'No!'

Scrambling to stop him, she put both hands on his shoulders and pushed hard. 'Stop. Dex. Stop!' She shoved at him and within the next instant they were both standing there, staring wide-eyed at each other.

'Iris?' Dex reached out a hand but she backed off. 'Don't.'

'Don't?' Confusion was written all over his face as they both struggled to gain control over their breathing. 'What's wrong?'

She couldn't look at him any more, couldn't look at the pleading in his eyes as his clouded brain tried to figure out what on earth was going on. Turning away, she forced her wooden legs to move, to put even more distance between them.

'You need to go.' Her words were as stilted as the way she walked.

'Iris. I don't understand.' When he tried to come closer, she spun on her heel and put both of her hands up in front of her.

'Stay back.' She shook her head as anger fought its way through to become the dominant emotion. She was angry with herself more than him. Angry that she'd allowed herself to give in to the feelings he evoked, angry that she'd let it go too far and angry that she'd shown him such a vulnerable side to herself.

'Just tell me what's going on.' He stood there, bewildered, confused and looking incredibly gorgeous. Iris closed her eyes, needing to shut out the sight of him because one look into those hypnotic brown eyes of his and she knew her anger would immediately dissipate. 'One second we're all hot and heavy and definitely on the same page and then…' He shrugged his shoulders.

'What? Your ego's dented because I've stopped you?'

Dex exhaled harshly. 'This has nothing to do with my ego, Iris.' Exasperation was written all over his face. 'I want to know what's going on inside you. What happened? That's all I'm asking.'

'So you can rationalise why a woman might reject you? I guess you're used to women just throwing themselves at your feet. Well, I'm not one of them.'

'Iris, this is ridiculous.' He spread his arms wide

as though he really couldn't get a grasp on what was happening. The woman had set him on fire like no other woman had. She'd been with him, step for step, moment for moment, and then— bam! Nothing. Nothing but anger and pain.

'You're darned right it is.'

'Tell me what I did. Did I do something wrong? Did I go too far too fast? If that's the case, I'm sorry. It's just that…' He stopped and raked a hand through his hair.

'What?'

How could he tell her that she was incredible? That for the first time he'd been able to kiss a woman and not have the distant memory of Catherine plaguing him in the background? The way he felt about Iris was powerful, possessive and passionate. 'You're…different.'

Her eyes widened at his words and a fresh wave of pain and embarrassment swamped her. She knew she was different. She was covered in scars and she knew it. What she didn't need was him pointing it out. She indicated to the door. 'Get. Out.'

'What?' If he'd been confused before, it was nothing compared to now. Why was she angry? His mind searched for an answer, a reason as to how she could have misconstrued his words.

'You're different, Iris, because you make me feel so much more than any oth—'

Iris didn't want to hear it. Didn't want to hear whatever lame-brained excuse he could come up with to try and fix the situation. She was a challenge to him, she could see that now. Make love to the elephant woman. Well, there'd be none of that. Not now. Not ever. If he wasn't going to leave, she'd do the next best thing. She'd *make* him go. She stalked to the bedroom, went in and slammed the door behind her, leaning against it to stop him from coming in.

'Iris.' His voice was muffled. 'Is it because of the scars? I don't care about your scars and when I said you were different, that wasn't what I meant.'

Iris put her hands over her ears as she slid to the floor. She didn't want to hear it. Didn't want to hear the excuses, the rationalisations, the lies. She just wanted him to go, to leave her alone. For ever.

On Tuesday, Iris returned from her first outing as part of the house-call team. She and Melissa had done what they'd termed 'the baby run'. They'd visited farms, driving to some and going via helicopter to others simply because there were so many women to review and so little time. Lots of pregnant women, lots of newborn babes and lots of children everywhere they went.

'That's been one of the best days I've had since arriving in Didja,' Iris declared as Melissa parked the ute next to the apartment block. She wondered whether that was because it had simply been herself and her friend or the fact that she hadn't had to worry about bumping into Dex.

'It was a great girly day,' Lis agreed. 'And now I think we deserve a treat.'

'Yeah?' Iris was interested. 'What might that be?'

'A nice cool drink at the pub and then delicious food at Stiggie's.'

'That does sound great.' The enthusiasm fell from Iris's voice but she smiled to encourage her friend. No doubt Melissa would want to catch up with Joss. After all, the man was her fiancé. If that was the case, the chance of Dex tagging along or being in one of the places Melissa was planning to visit would mean that it would end up being the four of them.

How was Iris supposed to keep her distance from Dex when he was not only Melissa's brother but Joss's best friend? She supposed she could plead an excuse and head indoors, holing up in her apartment for the night, but she'd done that too much recently and, besides, she wouldn't mind having a bit of time to unwind and relax with her friend.

If Dex joined them, well, she'd deal with it. She would be polite. She would be all ease and friendliness. She would not focus on the fact that she wished for his lips to be pressed to hers once more. She would not dwell on the way his hands had felt as they'd caressed her hair, her neck, her body and how, even though she was ugly and scarred, he'd wanted more.

She would not even dwell on the fact that she wished to be in a relationship again. That she longed to be special to someone as she'd been with Tim. Her body was scarred, it was horrible and twisted, and whilst she hated the sight of her flesh, Dex had openly declared that her scars didn't bother him.

Of course, she knew he'd had to be sweet-talking her but, still, it had been nice to actually hear those words. Unfortunately, those words had given her hope and she knew that one day that hope would come crashing down around her, hurting her once more. Hadn't she been hurt enough? Why couldn't she wish for a fairy-tale? One where a knight in shining armour galloped in on his white steed and swept her into his arms, returning them to his castle where he would take his time making slow and sweet love to the woman of his dreams.

Life wasn't fair.

'So?' Melissa was looking expectantly at her.

'Huh? Sorry. I was miles away.'

Lis smiled. 'I noticed. You had a far-off dreamy look on your face.' Lis nudged Iris. 'Not thinking about anyone in particular, eh? Someone like… my brother?'

'Dex? What? No way. He's too much a player for the likes of me. Playboys and scarred women don't mix.'

'How do you know until you try?' Melissa smiled and then continued. 'So? The pub?'

'Sure.'

'I'll just go put the medical bags and the files inside. See you in five minutes?'

'Sounds great.' Iris was pleased to have a few minutes alone. Too many thoughts. Too many thoughts of Dex, she corrected. Every time she heard his voice around the clinic, it made her warm with delight. Every time she caught a glimpse of him, whether it was smiling, laughing or pensive, it made her stomach flip-flop with excitement. Every time he looked at her as though he simply wanted to climb across the meeting-room desk and kiss her senseless her heart pounded with longing.

Why did she have to be attracted to him? Why him? What was it about Dex that held so much appeal when she knew he was so incredibly wrong for her? He was a playboy. He knew how to turn on the charm, to make her feel a certain way, to stick in her mind so she never stopped thinking about him.

Iris shook her head, not wanting to dwell on Dex right now. She was going to meet her good friend and cap off a brilliant day with a drink at the pub and a mouth-watering meal. With that, thoughts of Dexter Crawford were relegated to the back of her mind and shoved into a very small corner.

She met Melissa and the two of them set off for the pub. It was full to bursting when they arrived, the February day having been one of the hottest they'd experienced that year. Iris wasn't surprised to see Dex there, talking to two blonde girls. A pain of rejection and jealousy shot through her and she tried to look away.

Before she could, Dex surprised her further as she noticed that his hands were full of a stack of dirty glasses and within another moment he'd slipped behind the bar, put the dirties down and started pulling beers.

'What's Dex doing behind the bar?' she asked Melissa.

'Oh, he does that from time to time. He worked in a pub when he was in medical school so he knows what he's doing.'

Iris shook her head. The man became more and more intriguing with every passing moment.

'I'll get some drinks, you see if you can grab us a table,' Melissa said, and headed off before Iris could reply. She found a table and sat down, being joined within a few minutes by some locals, wanting to chat. Melissa returned with their drinks, Joss came and claimed most of his fiancée's attention, people talked, laughed and exchanged news, and all the while Iris kept glancing across to where Dex continued to work behind the bar.

He chatted with everyone. Men and women of all ages. The two blondes he'd been talking to when she'd first arrived were now talking to some of the miners. Dex didn't seem bothered at all. In fact, Iris was sure he didn't even give them a second glance. It didn't add up. If he was a playboy, wouldn't he be wanting to…do whatever it was he did? Instead, he was behind the bar, helping out.

Only when they were about ready to head to Stiggie's did Dex come on over.

Iris felt her heart pound at his nearness. Tried not to close her eyes as she breathed in his scent. Forced herself to stop staring at his lips as though she wanted nothing more than to have them back on hers.

'Ready?' Joss stood and helped Melissa to her feet.

'Dinner?' Iris asked, and wondered why her voice sounded deeper and huskier than usual. She cleared her throat, hoping no one would notice over the din. She glanced at Dex. Had he noticed? She was surprised to find him looking at her and his smile was wide and sexy.

'I'm starved,' he announced, not bothering to take his eyes from hers. Iris could feel her heart rate picking up speed as it had the other night. Now that she had a frame of reference, now that he'd held her in his arms, had pressed his mouth to hers, had caressed her face—every time she looked at him all she could concentrate on was finding a way to get him to repeat what they'd shared. It had been powerful. Mind-numbing. Heart-wrenching.

As they left the pub, walking down the road to the restaurant, Iris made sure she walked as far away from him as she could. It was insane how strong the attraction was between them but after the other night she should have realised it would intensify.

Dex had been well aware of Iris watching him as he'd worked behind the bar, feeling her gaze upon him, making his skin prickle with repressed excitement. They hadn't spoken about the other night, about how they'd felt so right in each other's arms. It had been an odd realisation and one Dex hadn't felt in an incredibly long time.

The feelings he had towards Iris were real. That knowledge alone had stunned him completely. He'd sat in his apartment the past few nights coming to terms with such a sensation. Iris, in his arms. Iris, touching his body. Iris, with her mouth wreaking havoc on all his senses. Good heavens. He wanted her now. He wanted her in his arms, the two of them, holding each other, their hearts pounding as one.

When Joss had suggested dinner, Dex had jumped at the chance. He'd tried to keep his distance from Iris around the clinic these past few days but now he felt like a man who had been crawling through a desert, circling an oasis. He needed to drink. He needed Iris as close as possible to him. If dinner with Joss and Lis was all he could get, he'd take it.

As they were seated by Stig himself, Dex was delighted to find himself sitting opposite Iris. Looking across at her was something he found very pleasing, and as they ordered, he could see her visibly start to relax. Had she thought Lis and Joss might find an excuse to leave? Had she been concerned she might be left all alone to dine with him?

They placed their orders and settled into easy conversation, as the evening progressed, Iris began to relax even more. The food was fantastic, the company was relaxing and Dex was pleased he'd made her laugh on more than one occasion. Iris was relaxed…at least she was until just before dessert when Joss stood.

'Thanks for dinner.' He held out his hand to Melissa. 'Sorry to eat and run but we have to get going.'

'Why?' Melissa stood, voicing the question which was on Iris's lips.

'Because I have a special surprise set up for

the two of us,' Joss remarked as he placed his arm around Melissa. 'Thanks for dinner. Have a nice dessert.'

Once again the two lovebirds swept out of the place in such a whirlwind that Iris glared open-mouthed at Dex. 'What just happened?' she asked.

'They left,' Dex replied. 'And left me to foot the bill.' He shook his head.

'I can pay for my meal,' she offered, and received a dazzling smile from Dex. 'What?' Iris asked, feeling highly self-conscious when he simply kept looking at her like that.

'Your independence.'

'What about it?'

'It reminds me of the first day we met. When I tried to buy you a hat.'

'One with corks.'

Dex chuckled and the deep sound washed over her. Iris closed her eyes, trying to pull herself together. She was sitting in a restaurant, a lit candle on the table between them, trying to ignore the pounding of her heart as the town's leading bachelor created havoc with her system.

'You would have looked good with corks all around. Would have made kissing you nigh impossible but—'

Her eyes snapped open. 'I knew I should have bought it,' she interrupted, anger rising at the way he was charming her. Good. She liked anger. When she was angry with Dex, she was better able to hide her own emotions.

'Come on. Was kissing me so bad?' He raised an eyebrow as he leaned back in his chair to look at her.

'I don't want to talk about it.' Iris started fumbling in her purse for some money and stood, throwing some bills onto the table, not caring if it was accurate or not. 'I have to go.'

'Wait. Iris.' Dex copied her action, leaving money for Stig before rushing out after her. 'Iris.' He caught up to her in a few easy strides. 'I take it you don't want dessert?'

'No. Thank you.' Especially if *he* was on the menu. She needed to get as far away from him as possible because even through her anger she could feel the desperate need rising to have his mouth over hers once more. Why was his hold over her so powerful? Why couldn't she fight it?

They passed the pub and the rowdy noise still coming from it.

'And what was with you tonight in the pub?' she questioned hotly, the words tumbling out without much thought. That was also a problem. When she was around him and feeling that unmistakable pull, all her good sense and reason seemed to disappear into thin air.

'What are you talking about?'

'You were clearing glasses and pulling beers and mixing drinks.'

'I know how.' He shrugged as though it was no big deal. 'I help out quite frequently, especially when it's so stinking hot every man and his dog comes in for a drink.'

'But you weren't chatting up any of your usual beauty queens. Trying out your lines. Keeping yourself fresh and available for the ladies.'

'Oh.' He drawled the word slowly. His own temper started to rise but he kept it in check. 'So that's what this is about. Other women.' They'd arrived at the apartments now and Iris fished inside her bag for her keys but her hands were fumbling so badly she stopped for a moment, hoping to regain some control over her faculties.

'You're a playboy, Dex. It's what you do. All I'm saying is I was surprised tonight *not* to see you doing it.'

'No. What you're *really* saying, Iris, is that now that I've kissed you, I should be moving on to my next conquest. You want to see me with other women so you can point the finger and tell me how right you were, that your judgement of me was correct. That I am a dyed-in-the-wool playboy.

'Well, you're wrong, sweetheart. There is more to me than meets the eye, only you're too blind to see it. You're too busy worrying about your scars to see that other people have their own problems. We've all had bad relationships. We've all had deep emotional trauma and we all deal with it in completely different ways. If I choose to lose myself in the smile of a pretty woman, that's my prerogative. If I choose to help out behind a bar, making life easier for one of my mates, that's my prerogative.'

He stepped closer, so their bodies were almost touching. 'If I choose to haul you into my arms…' As he spoke, he acted out the words, making Iris's heart hammer wildly in her chest, her mouth dry, her mind blank save for how he made her feel. 'And kiss you so deeply we both forget the pain of our pasts, then—'

He didn't get to finish his sentence as Iris urged his head down, their mouths melding and fusing together with such intensity it shocked them both.

The heat, the passion, the power of what they wanted, what they were giving and taking, was filled with pure mutual need. She had never been kissed like this before. Even the other night he'd started out slowly and then after a while the need had overwhelmed both of them.

This time, however, there was nothing but a basic animalistic force driving them both forward, pushing them beyond their boundaries. His arms were wrapped around her tightly, holding her as close to his body as he could get, whilst her hands wound around his neck, her fingers in his hair as she made sure he didn't, for any reason whatsoever, stop this incredible torture he was subjecting her to.

Heat. Passion. Power.

They were on fire, unable to get enough and desperate for more. Nothing mattered any more. Not the hurtful words they'd said to each other, not the logic dictating they were all wrong for each other and not the scars on her body which had previously kept them from each other.

This was right. The rest of the world was wrong. Time stood still and raw hunger grew.

'Iris.' Her name was on his mouth as he tore it from hers, both of them sucking in air. 'You are…incredible.'

She pulled his mouth back to hers, not wanting

to hear the words. The actions of his attraction were far more easy to believe than his words telling her she was beautiful when she knew quite clearly she was not. Besides, when his mouth was on hers like this, she couldn't think. Didn't want to think. Simply wanted to absorb. Simply wanted to forget about her past, her scars and focus on the way Dex made her feel. Hot, sexy and powerful. It was all wrong yet it felt so right.

Talking was out of the question. That much she'd made clear and at the moment Dex wasn't one to argue. He'd tried to tell her before that she was different from other women and he most certainly hadn't been talking about her scars. The way she made *him* feel was different from other women. He hadn't wanted to talk to any of those women in the bar tonight because none of them were Iris. That was the truth of the matter and in turn it only brought a larger succession of thoughts to plague him.

It was clear that Iris was as attracted to him as he was to her. What they were doing right now was evidence of that, but was she only using him? She'd marked him as a playboy and, therefore, perhaps she thought she could wipe away thoughts of her husband, thoughts of her past by losing herself in him? The thought left him feeling hollow and as though he was competing against a ghost, which was ridiculous.

If he pursued this attraction, if they let it take its course, there was no telling where they'd end up. Iris was relationship material and he didn't do that. He'd been crushed by Catherine all those years ago but right now Iris had more power to hurt him and he didn't like that thought at all. He didn't do relationships simply because he knew he'd fail. He knew at some point he'd let her down, hurt her, and he couldn't. She was too special for that.

'Iris.' He edged back again, sucking in oxygen from the warm evening air, the summer sun now almost set. 'Iris. We need to talk.'

Her answer was to urge his head back to hers. Dex kissed her again but this time managed to pull superhuman strength from somewhere and temper his need. His mouth wasn't as hard on hers as before yet hers was, urging him forward, wanting him back where they'd both just been.

'Iris.' This time when he spoke her name she stopped and pulled herself from his arms, her breathing as erratic as his.

'Talk. Right. We…uh…need to talk.' Her words

came out in gasps as she desperately tried to get herself under control.

'We do.' He indicated the door behind her. 'Do you want to go inside?'

'To talk?' She looked at him as though he'd just grown an extra head. 'After *that* kiss?' She shook her head. 'I don't think that's a good idea, Dex. Besides, you obviously have something to say, so I think you should come right out and say it.'

'It's not that I…want to say…' He stopped and raked a hand through his hair, his body still on fire from the best kiss of his life. 'I just think we need to talk about what's going on between us. That's all.'

'Why? Because you don't want it?' She shook her head. 'You don't have to worry about that because I don't want it, either. I'm only in Didja until the middle of the year and then I leave. I have another job lined up, remember?'

'I remember. Listen, it's not that I don't find—'

'It's clear we have an attraction but we're also mature enough not to let it rule us…as it did just now. We'll be stronger. Better able to be around each other at work and avoid each other everywhere else. Deal?' Iris had collected her bag which had dropped unnoticed to the ground when she'd been unable to control the urge to kiss Dex.

Now she had her keys in her hand and inserted the key into the lock, pleased her hands weren't trembling as much as the rest of her body.

'Iris—'

'Good,' she said, answering her own question, and without giving him the opportunity to respond any further she opened her door and slipped inside.

Dex was once more left standing outside her apartment, looking at the closed door, knowing it was for the best but for some reason not liking it one little bit.

CHAPTER EIGHT

THREE days later, Iris had just finished up her Friday clinic and was getting ready to lock up her consulting room when the phone rang. She automatically picked it up.

'Dr Tennant.'

'Is that Dr Iris Tennant?' It was a woman's voice on the other end of the line and one Iris didn't recognise.

'Yes.'

'I'm calling from Missionary World Aid. I'm afraid I have some rather bad news.'

Iris's mouth went dry and she sank down into her chair as she listened to what the woman had to say. Her friends Nigel and Francie, who had been working as missionaries in Tarparnii, had been killed in a car accident. Their eight-month-old daughter, Anya, however, was fine as she hadn't been in the car with them.

'As the registered guardian for little Anya, we

were wanting to arrange a meeting to sign the necessary documents.'

Guardian? Documents? Iris's mind went completely blank for a second before she snapped back into professional mode. 'Where is Anya?'

'She's currently at a foster-home in Perth.'

Iris took notes. Wrote things down but was completely numb. When she replaced the phone, she sat there, looking out into nothingness. When a knock came at her door, she didn't flinch, she didn't say a thing. A moment later, the door opened and Dex stuck his head around.

'You are in here. Good. Do you have David Toonamon's notes?' Dex walked further into the room and frowned. 'Iris?' The look on her face was one of shocked incredulity mixed with a healthy portion of pain. He knew the look well because he was sure he'd had an identical one on his face when he'd first discovered he was adopted. It didn't matter what was or wasn't happening between them. Iris needed a friend and he still prided himself on being that. 'Iris, what's happened?'

'They're dead.'

It wasn't what he'd expected her to say. He walked around her desk and swivelled her chair so she was facing him. Melissa and Joss were out doing house calls again and a strange dark sensation started curling in the pit of his stomach. They were due back any minute and Dex held his breath as he looked intently into her green eyes. 'Who? Iris? Tell me who?'

'Francie and Nigel.'

Dex slowly released the air which had built up in his lungs. Not Melissa and Joss. Now he could step back and help Iris. 'Friends of yours?'

'Yes. Missionaries. Tarparnii.' She was looking straight ahead, unable to focus properly. She was in shock even though her brain was probably ticking over too fast to process everything clearly.

'What happened?'

'Car accident. Both dead. No foul play. Both dead.' She shook her head. 'Why does this happen to me? The people I love, the people I care about.' Iris swallowed, waiting for the tears to fall, but they didn't come.

Dex remembered her mentioning these people before. Not their names but on her first day here, at the fair, she'd mentioned her missionary friends. She also said they had a small baby. 'What about their baby?'

The look she gave him was one of blankness. 'The baby?'

'Didn't they have a child? A young baby? You bought a present for her. A soft toy. Remember?'

Iris slowly closed her eyes as though the pain was just too much to bear. 'Anya. She wasn't in the car. She's in Perth.' Iris opened her eyes and Dex saw fear reflected there. 'They want me to go and get her, Dex.'

'Why?'

'I'm her guardian.'

'You're her…' He stopped and stood back, breathing out slowly.

'Guardian. I have guardianship of a baby.' Her eyes were wild. 'What am I supposed to do, Dex?'

'You're her…' Even he was having trouble saying the words.

'Guardian.' Iris shook her head, her breathing starting to become uneven. 'I can't look after a child. I'm not qualified for that.'

'You're a paediatrician, Iris,' he felt compelled to point out. 'You know how children work.'

'Yes. How they work. Exactly. I know how to fix them, to mend them when they're broken, to give them back to their parents.' She spread her arms wide. 'I don't have the first clue about how to raise one, how to do…things with them.' She shook her head. 'I can't do this. I can't do this.'

Her breathing had increased and he realised she was starting to hyperventilate. Dex immediately pushed her head between her knees. 'Breathe. Just breathe. It's OK. It'll be OK.'

She raised her head to look at him. 'Which part of this is OK?'

'Shh.' He put her head back down. 'Just…concentrate on your breathing for now. You just need to calm down and think things through. Everything's just a bit of a shock right now. That's all. You're a strong woman. You can do this. You'll figure it out.'

Iris closed her eyes, allowing his soothing words to wash over her. His voice was so nice, so rich, so calming.

'Just breathe.'

She sucked in air and slowly her breathing began to return to a more normal pace, the immediate anxiety starting to dissipate. Lifting her head, she looked at Dex who was crouched down next to her chair.

'There. Better.'

'You have the most calming voice. So soft and smooth. Like silk. It just washes over you.'

They were close. Close enough that if he were to lean forward a touch, he'd be able to kiss

those luscious lips of hers. He stared at her
mouth, wanting to feel those same sensations
he'd experienced last week. 'You shouldn't say
things like that.'

'It's the truth.'

'I'm trying to keep my distance here, Iris. I'm
trying to figure out what on earth it is that I feel
for you, why I'm finding it increasingly difficult
to get you out of my mind, and you certainly don't
make it any easier when you say things like that.'

'I'm sorry.' Her eyes were filled with sincerity.
'About last week. About everything. I was rude.
I treated you badly. Not just once but twice. I'm
sorry, Dex.'

Dex stood, needing to put distance between
them because if he didn't he wasn't sure he'd be
able to control himself at all. The way her eyes
intensified with green warmth when she spoke
like that, the way her own sultry tones filled him
with anticipation, the way her fresh, springtime
scent wove its way into his senses. The woman
was undeniably gorgeous and resisting her was
becoming one of the daily battles he faced.

During the last few days Iris hadn't spoken to
him unless it had been in direct relation to a patient
or something to do with the running of the clinic,

and he'd decided to respect her decision and follow her lead. They were like chalk and cheese and were better off remaining simply colleagues.

But now this had happened.

Dex had happened on her only a moment after she'd received such terrible and distressing news and that was why she was now saying what she was saying. She was grateful for his assistance and, therefore, she needed to put things right between them. She'd had a shock and sometimes a shock could help your perspective to shift, just a touch, so you could see the world in a completely different light. When she figured out what she wanted to do, she'd probably regret apologising to him, regret showing so much of her soul. She'd made it clear that she only thought of him as the town's resident playboy and she was here for less than five more months. She had her next job all lined up and come the end of July, she would leave Didja.

Now, though, it appeared her life was once again to be thrust into turmoil. She'd just discovered she was guardian to a small baby. Even he was having trouble wrapping his head around the concept so it must be infinitely more difficult for Iris. Not only that, her good friends had passed away and death was never easy to deal with.

Her life was changing and even if for one solitary moment he'd contemplated being a part of it, he realised as he looked at her that it could never be. Not now. She would have a child to care for. He would support her in a professional capacity, he'd be polite and helpful, but apart from that, Iris Tennant was now officially off-limits to him.

He walked around to the other side of her desk, needing even more space, to put more physical as well as mental distance between them. 'What are you going to do?'

Iris looked away from him. She'd been trying to apologise for her bad behaviour, for allowing her neuroses to rule her life. She'd been so wrapped up in her own problems that she'd forgotten that there was a bigger picture out there. Well, if he didn't want to accept her apology, that was fine. She would just move on. Take the next step. Figure out what to do now.

'I guess I'll go to Perth. Meet with the foster-mother and the solicitors.' She shook her head again. 'I'm a guardian. It sounds so strange to say it out loud. I simply never thought it through, you know. When they asked me to be guardian, to be Anya's godmother, of course I accepted. I mean, I love Francie. She's a good friend of mine and so is Nigel. But I never expected them to…' She stopped, still unable to get her head around the fact that they were gone. Gone from her life. Gone from their daughter's life. Just like that.

'You'll need to go to Perth.' Dex started to pace the room. 'Do you have anywhere to stay when you get there?'

Iris frowned. 'Hotel.' She shrugged. 'I'll just get a room somewhere. The other thing I'm not sure of is how long all of this is going to take. I mean, I don't want to leave Joss in the lurch, or the people of Didja. This community has been so welcoming to me.' Iris turned in her chair, unable to look at him, unable to think about leaving this warm outback township so soon.

'Don't go fretting about the clinic, and you do have a six-month contract, Iris. We won't let you break it that easily.'

'We?'

Dex stopped pacing and put his hands into his pockets. 'Joss and myself.'

'What about Melissa?'

'Well, I'm sure she'd want you to stick around too, but I mean from a contractual point of view. This is what small clinics are like. We can work around each other's needs.'

'You keep saying "we".'

Dex frowned for a second. 'You do know that Joss and I own the clinic. We're partners. Financially as well as professionally.'

'Wha…?' Iris knew her mouth was hanging open but within a split second she had recovered. 'No. Actually, I didn't know that.' Again it showed her another side to Dex. One of responsibility, of giving to the community, of being a businessman. 'I'm sorry. I thought Joss owned the clinic.'

'Joss started the clinic but not long after I arrived here, he wanted to expand so I invested. Joss is much better at the day-to-day running of everything, taking command of the ship, so to speak, so I just leave him to it.'

Now it all made perfect sense as to why Dex had read her résumé. Why he'd been able to discover her marital status. It also meant he'd be able to help her out in this situation.

'Are you saying, then, that you don't want me to break my contract, that you're more than happy for me to take some time off, to go to Perth to sort this out and then bring a small baby back here and continue with my contract of providing paediatric care to Didja's community?'

Dex grinned and nodded. 'That's exactly what I'm saying.'

'You'd…do that?' Especially after the way she'd treated him? Iris was astounded at the immediate generosity of the man before her.

'Hey. You've got to sort your life out somewhere and Didja is as good a place as any. Besides, do you have any idea just how Bub will feel about having to look after a little baby whilst you consult? She'll be beside herself with joy.'

'Oh.' Iris frowned. 'I hadn't even thought that far.' She shook her head. 'It's all happening too fast. My mind is a blur. My thoughts are all jumbled, jumping over each other, trying to be the one I listen to first.'

'Sounds like sheep at drenching time.' Dex chuckled but then quickly sobered. What they were discussing here was important and could well affect the rest of Iris's life. He started to pace the floor again but they were interrupted by the arrival of Joss and Melissa. They both came into Iris's consulting room.

'What are you two both doing here at this time of night? There are no patients in the waiting room and Areva's about to close up shop,' Melissa remarked.

'How were house calls?' Dex asked, although

he didn't sound as though he was at all interested in the answer.

'Fine. No dramas. Lots of pregnant women. All healthy with growing babes inside them.' Melissa smiled brightly at them both. 'And what's been going on here today? Anything of interest?'

Iris nodded slowly and met her friend's gaze.

'What is it?' Melissa was instantly alert, looking from Iris to Dex and back again.

'It's Francie and Nigel.' Iris slowly explained what she'd just been told on the phone and after Melissa had hugged her tightly and Joss had offered his condolences, he shifted straight into business mode.

'Dex is right. You must go to Perth and sort this out. Tomorrow.'

'But, I'm supposed to do—'

'We can cover whatever clinics, whatever patients you might have needed to see,' Melissa soothed. 'This community rallies around its own and no one will mind waiting a bit longer for their children to see you.'

'We're a family,' Joss reiterated. 'We stick together.'

'Yeah,' Dex chimed in. 'And when you're in Perth, you could even stay with Joss's parents. That way, you're not facing these big decisions on your own or going back to an impersonal hotel room.'

'Dex is right.' Joss nodded. 'My parents would be only too happy to help…' He stopped and shook his head. 'Actually. No, they won't. I was speaking to my dad only last night and he has really bad summer flu. Hasn't been well for weeks and neither of them told me. Not good for you or a small baby.'

'It's all right. I don't mind the hotel. That way I'm not putting anyone out,' Iris ventured, although she knew she could really do with some support during this traumatic and emotional time. Still, she'd come through worse on her own and she would soldier on through this.

'No.' Melissa shook her head. 'You need support. This is too big for you to face on your own.' She thought for a moment. 'I know, why don't you stay with Dexter's parents?' Melissa ventured.

'What?' Dex was stunned at this suggestion.

'It makes sense.' Joss stepped protectively next to his fiancée and placed his arm about Melissa's waist. 'Your parents have been through similar circumstances. They'd probably be able to give Iris a helping hand with the decision-making process.'

'But…you just can't…' He stopped and glared

at Joss. 'You know the relationship I have with my parents. You can't expect me just to call them up out of the blue and ask if a colleague can crash at their place whilst she wrestles with some major life-changing decisions.'

Joss shook his head. 'I never expected you to do that. I was going to call them and ask, and it wouldn't be out of the blue.'

Dex's tone dropped, his words very quiet. 'What is that supposed to mean? Have you been in contact with my parents?'

'Yes.'

'For how long?'

'Ever since you arrived here.' Joss met his friend's gaze fair and square. Iris felt as though she should jump between them to stop them from coming to blows with each other but right now she honestly didn't think she'd be all that effective. 'They're your parents, Dex. They love you. They always have.'

'They lied to me.' They'd taken his happy, carefree childhood and smashed it into a million pieces. He hadn't been able to cope, hadn't been able to believe his entire life had been one huge lie. It had made him realise that if he couldn't cope with his own life being shattered, he never wanted to put himself in such a vulnerable position as marriage in case he ended up being tested once again.

'A mistake they've regretted more than once.'

Melissa was the first one to move. She walked over to Dex's side and placed her hand on his arm. 'It's time, Dex. Time to forgive, to forget.' Iris watched as Melissa soothed Dex instantly and realised that whilst Dex might not think there was a very strong bond between them, he was obviously wrong. His sister knew him far better than he perhaps realised. 'Let go of the pain and move forward. You know that your parents can help Iris and you're the type of man who likes to help others. It's in you. I've seen it time and time again.'

'This is a conspiracy,' he said, but his words were nowhere near as vehement as before.

'That's one way to look at it.' Joss nodded at his friend. 'Lis is right. You know it. I know it. It's time to go home, Dex.'

'Take Iris. Support her. Be there for her.'

Iris was about to protest but found she couldn't. What she was facing was more than she'd bargained for and if she was going to be honest, she'd admit that she was in way over her head.

'I never thought they'd die. I never thought,

when I agreed to be Anya's guardian, that this would happen.' The words were spoken softly as she looked at Dex. 'When Tim died, I realised so much of the silly things in life we stress and fret over don't really mean anything. Perspectives shift and that phone call has shifted mine. I do need help and that isn't an easy thing for me to admit. If you're offering your support, Dex, I accept.'

Dex looked around the room at the people he called friends, family and colleagues. He wanted to help Iris. More than anything. He wanted to support her as she hadn't really allowed him to support her the other night. Sure, things had got out of hand but he was positive he now had himself under control where the attraction between them was concerned.

Still, in supporting Iris, did that mean he had to see his parents? Could he do it? Melissa and Joss were right saying that his parents, the two people who had been through the adoption process, would be able to help Iris with the enormous decision facing her.

If he was honest with himself, he'd admit that he'd known this time would come, that he had felt it drawing closer. Hadn't he been thinking about Mason and Xandi more often lately?

Hadn't he even toyed with the idea of perhaps contacting his siblings to see how they were? And now Joss was telling him that the door between himself and his family wasn't completely shut—it had been kept ajar.

He was filled with dread mixed with excitement. Apprehension mixed with fear. Stubbornness mixed with hope.

Dex sucked in a deep breath and slowly let it out. Perspectives shifted. When he'd come to Didja, his perspective had been very inward looking. Two years later and he was facing strong emotional feelings for a woman he was determined to resist. However, being around Iris, realising the trauma she'd been through, the nightmares that still plagued her…it had made his own problems seem minute in comparison. Now that strong, independent woman was asking for his help but she wanted him to offer it willingly. He looked directly at Iris and nodded slowly.

'I'm definitely offering.'

CHAPTER NINE

THEY stood outside the front door of the house, Iris looking up at the impressive large wooden carved door, Dex looking down at his feet.

'Your home is enormous.' She couldn't help the words that came from her mouth unbidden. Dex glanced at her, about to tell her that this wasn't his home, that it was simply a place owned by his adoptive parents, but the words died on his lips.

It was his home. It was the place he'd called home for over thirty years. It was the place that held so many memories, some good, some bad. He remembered falling off his tricycle just over to the left near the hedge. He remembered climbing out the back second-storey bedroom window onto the bough of a tree when he was a teenager. He remembered walking out the very door they now stood in front of, vowing never to return.

'I don't know if I can do this.' The words were barely a whisper and Iris did the only thing she could do to help him, to reassure him, to show him that just as he'd offered to be there to support her in her time of need, she would be there to support him.

She reached out and took his hand in hers.

Dex was surprised at the action yet incredibly pleased at the same time. For a woman who didn't like to be touched, who shied away from physical contact, it was definitely a milestone and one she'd chosen to share with him. The fact that he'd held her in his arms on several occasions, the fact that he'd pressed his mouth to hers in the most electrifying kisses he'd ever experienced, the fact that she'd let him press kisses to her delectable body didn't mean the same as the simple gesture she offered now.

Reaching out and holding his hand was Iris's way of letting him know how much she really cared about him. This moment wasn't about sexual attraction, this moment was about support. He'd known throughout his relationship with Catherine that he'd been the giver and she'd been the taker. She had never supported him. She'd never encouraged him and she'd certainly never asked for his help.

Iris had done all those things and Dex looked

at her, his fear lifting when he saw that she truly believed he was strong enough to go through with this reconciliation. She was an amazing woman.

'You can do this, Dex.' Her words were sure and firm. 'I'm right here for whatever you need.'

A rakish grin immediately lit his features and he waggled his eyebrows up and down. 'Whatever I need?'

Instead of getting angry, instead of pulling away from him, Iris smiled shyly. 'You know what I mean.'

She realised his teasing was also a cover-up for his true feelings and she wondered how many other times he'd employed such a tactic. At any rate, she'd come to the conclusion during the drive from Didja to Kalgoorlie and then on the plane from Kalgoorlie to Perth that trying to fight her increasing attraction to Dex as well as accepting the enormous events that were presently happening in her life was just too much to handle. She liked Dex. She liked the way he teased her and she liked the way he made her feel when he looked at her the way he was now.

She liked him. She really liked him and that in itself was a miracle. After Tim's death, she'd vowed never to fall in love again, never to give her heart to a man, never to trust her emotions to one single person. Yet four years later here she was. Standing next to a man who had come to mean a great deal to her. Holding his hand. Helping him just as he was helping her.

Although admitting to herself that she liked Dex didn't necessarily mean she wanted to get serious about the emotions he could stir up simply with one of his sexy looks but accepting there might be something a little more than friendship between them was the easier option to take at the moment.

'Yeah.' He leaned a little closer. 'I know what you mean.' Before she could blink, he stole a quick kiss from her lips. The brief butterfly touch created more havoc with her system. The man was so addictive.

'Dex!' she whispered.

'What?'

'You have to stop doing that.' She raised her free hand to her lips and was surprised to find the exceedingly brief touch had left her trembling.

'Why? You have the most gorgeous mouth, Iris. So sweet, so full, so tempting.'

'Oh. Well…uh…then…*try* to resist.' As she spoke, she leaned forward and rang the doorbell. At least the banter, the teasing, the sneaking of kisses had helped to soothe him a little. The tension in his fingers, which were laced with hers, was less intense than before.

'I don't know. I've been resisting you for a while now, Iris. I'd even managed to convince myself that it would only be friendship between us. However, seeing this more…personal side of you is doing strange things to me.' Although there was a teasing glint in those big brown eyes of his, there was also an underlying hint of seriousness. He grinned as he spoke yet his body language said he was more serious than he was revealing. Unfortunately, she found it difficult to believe he was one hundred per cent serious. Still, those eyes of his were… And the way his mouth curved upwards made her want to…

Iris shook her head slowly as her smile increased. 'You're incorrigible, Dexter Crawford.'

'I'm inclined to agree with you, dear.'

Both of them snapped their heads to look at the woman who had spoken, the woman who stood before them, framed in the doorway.

'Mum!' The word was torn from him before he could think.

'Dex.' Mrs Crawford stood her ground, not moving, not wanting to push things too far too fast, but Iris could clearly see the emotions bubbling just beneath the surface. She looked at Dex and saw that he, too, was working hard at controlling himself.

'You look…' He stopped and dragged in a shaky breath. She looked older, more fragile, more worried than she had a right to. He swallowed, his Adam's apple moving up and down. Iris gave his hand a little squeeze of encouragement then let go. An instant later Dex had enveloped his mother in an enormous hug, the tears Mrs Crawford had been working hard at controlling bursting forth as she embraced her son for the first time in over two years.

Iris raised a hand to her mouth, trying to control her own emotions due to the privilege of witnessing such an intense, private moment between Dex and his mother.

'I only dreamed this day would come,' she whispered into his chest as he held her. 'I love you so much, Dexter. I always have. I'm so sorry, darling. I'm so sorry we hurt you.'

Dex didn't say anything for a moment and Iris could sense he was as choked up as his mother, but being a brave, strong man, he pulled himself together and broke the embrace, smiling down at his mother as he wiped her tears away. 'Shh. It's all good, Mum.' And it was, he realised. The moment he'd been dreading for so long had come and gone and he had to say he felt much freer than he had in years.

It was Mrs Crawford who looked past Dex and smiled through her tears. 'And this must be Iris. Oh, my dear, welcome, welcome.' She held out her free hand to Iris, the other one holding her son's as though she'd never let him go again.

'Thank you,' Iris murmured, and shook Mrs Crawford's hand.

'Look at us standing in the doorway like this. So silly. Come on in. Both of you.' Mrs Crawford tugged them forward. Iris's shoulder bag fell to her arm and she quickly righted it. Dex reached back for his own bag on the ground but his mother wasn't having any of it.

'Don't worry about your bag. We can get it later or your father can get that. Dwayne!' she hollered, still holding firmly onto Dex. 'Put your bag down there Iris. We'll show you to your room later on. Dwayne!' Mrs Crawford called again, and this time received a muffled reply. 'He's been out in his workshop, hammering and banging.' She looked pointedly at Iris. 'Never marry an inventor, dear. It doesn't matter how old they get, they never stop inventing. Anyway, he knew you were arriving around this time so he should— Ah, here he is.'

Father and son shook hands warmly and only when Dwayne pulled Dex forward into a big, manly hug did Mrs Crawford let go of her son's hand. It was a little odd but Iris found herself looking for similarities between the two men and whilst they were about the same height, nothing physical about them matched at all. However, as they stood in the entrance way, talking for a few moments, she noted that both men had the same mannerisms. The way they put their hands in their pockets or gestured with their eyebrows as they spoke. It was quite uncanny.

'Come in, Iris,' Mrs Crawford urged. 'Sit down. You must be exhausted after all that travelling. Joss said you were driving from Didja to Kalgoorlie and then catching the plane from there to Perth and then, of course, you had to get a taxi from the airport to here so all in all a rather long day, I'd say.'

'It's all been quite comfortable,' Iris managed as she sat on the comfortable sofa. 'I don't think I would have managed on my own. My mind would have been playing through every scenario

I could think of, but thankfully I had Dex not only to amuse me but distract my thoughts as well.'

'Ah…' She smiled at her son. 'I see he hasn't lost his touch for putting people at ease.'

Iris smiled brightly. 'Oh, he still has that. In abundance.'

'Good to hear. Now, dear, you must tell us all about yourself.'

'Mum,' Dex protested as he and his father came into the room. 'Don't badger her.' He sat down next to Iris on the sofa, both of them sitting on the edge, both of them a little uncomfortable but for very different reasons.

'It's all right, Dex,' Iris remarked as both his parents looked at her expectantly. 'First, Mr and Mrs Crawford, I'd like to thank you both for allowing me to stay with you whilst I'm in Perth.'

'Call me Ruth,' his mother protested.

'And I'm Dwayne.' He held out his hand to her and shook it almost as warmly as he had his son's.

'We don't stand on ceremony here. Besides, you're family. Anyone who works with Dex and Joss is automatically a part of us.'

'Well…thank you, Ruth.' Iris was touched. Never before, even with Tim's parents, had she felt so instantly at home. She eased back a little on the sofa as they started to chat. For the next hour, as they shared afternoon tea, Iris was acutely aware of Dex sitting incredibly close to her. The warmth of his arm brushing hers now and then. The pressure of his firm thigh against her own. That earthy, heady scent he wore almost drugging her senses it was so good.

By the time his siblings returned from university, Iris was more than ready to put some much-needed distance between herself and Dex. Ruth showed her to her room on the upper floor and when the door was closed, Iris sank gratefully down onto the comfortable bed.

She lay there for quite some time, her mind still whirring with everything that had happened during the past few days. She still hadn't managed to cry for Francie and Nigel, their loss still not seeming real.

It was an odd feeling, literally being left holding the baby. She knew Francie and Nigel had been wealthy and Anya would one day inherit everything so there was no need to worry about providing for the little one. She could also make sure Anya was raised with a firm understanding about wealth. Money could be a powerful motivator. It had certainly motivated Tim.

Iris hadn't thought it a problem at the beginning of their marriage because, of course, everyone wanted to have a nice place to live and a flashy car to drive. They'd both been earning good incomes and so Tim had argued that they should get the things they'd always dreamed of having whilst they were young and fit enough to enjoy them.

And it hadn't been a problem—until he'd lost his life trying to save their perishable possessions. Had he loved money more than her? Had he truly been motivated by it? Iris sighed, not that sure anymore. Tim was in her past and whilst she would always love him, she'd changed a lot in the last four years.

In fact, she'd changed a lot in the past five weeks. Didja, the people, the way they lived their lives, her colleagues…everything. Everything about the community had changed her. Yes, the pace of living was slower but wasn't that a good thing? Since she'd been cleared from her burns specialist to return to work, she'd been going non-stop…and slowly wasting away inside.

She could admit that now. She could see how empty her life had been and how things were subtly changing. Dex was obviously a big part of that. He'd held her when she'd cried. He'd picked up the pieces of the vase she'd smashed and seen her at her lowest. He'd kissed her. She closed her eyes at the memory of their shared kisses and just how he'd made her feel. She knew he felt something for her as well but lately she was getting mixed signals from him. Not that she blamed him. They'd both been running hot and cold, unsure of exactly where they stood. That was until she'd needed him and Dex had been there. Sure and strong.

When she had just started dating Tim, she'd asked her mother that all-important question… how do I know if I'm really in love? If he's truly the man for me? Her mother had replied in her matter-of-fact tone, 'You know he'll be yours for ever if you can imagine him changing your catheter bag when you're old and grey.'

She'd laughed at her mother's words but hadn't taken them seriously. She knew it wasn't that much of a challenge for doctors as they came into contact with things like catheter bags every day, but now her mother's words started to make more sense. Support was what her mother had really been talking about. Someone to support you through the darkest times of life.

Since she'd heard she was Anya's guardian,

Dex had been nothing but supportive. She'd been jittery when they'd initially set out but he hadn't pressured her on anything but supported her in everything. As they'd disembarked from the plane and taken a taxi to his parents' house, it had been her turn to be there to support him.

Dex hadn't spoken much, not until they'd been standing outside the front door. She'd known all along how difficult it was for him to face his past, to see his parents and siblings again, and he'd stood strong and firm next to her, making her laugh, stealing kisses, but he'd still gone through with it. He hadn't backed down. Once he'd made and accepted the decision to come home, he'd followed through, which showed he had immense courage.

When the knock came at her door, Iris quickly got up and looked at the clock. Almost an hour had passed since she'd sought solitude in the lavishly furnished bedroom. Where had the time gone? She smoothed her hair back, tucking a few loose strands behind her ears before opening the door.

'Hi.' Dex rushed into the room and shut the door behind him, not waiting for her to invite him in and almost knocking Iris over in the process.

'What's wrong?'

'What?' He tried to affect nonchalance. 'What

makes you think any thing's wrong?' he asked in
an overly bright voice, which sounded nothing at
all like Dex.

'Uh…possibly because you're acting really
weird.' She went and sat on the bed. Dex slumped
to the floor, his shoulders hanging dejectedly.

'I can't do this, Iris.'

'What? You've *done*, it Dex. You've recon-
nected with your family.'

'But that's just it. I haven't.'

'What are you talking about? It was hugs and
kisses and welcome home prodigal son when I
came in here.'

'Aha. I knew it. You left me out there on purpose
to be fed to the lions.'

She looked at him as though he'd grown an
extra head. 'I thought you all might appreciate a
bit of privacy. You know, family bonding time,
without needing to feel uncomfortable around
the stranger.'

Dex lifted his head and looked at her solemnly.
'You're not a stranger, Iris.'

'I am to them. I just thought a bit of privacy was
in order and I was feeling a little exhausted from
such a busy day.'

'No worse than doing house calls.'

'Whatever. It's irrelevant. What *is* relevant, however, is why you're hiding in here, declaring you can't do "this"? What exactly is "this" that you can't do?'

'Reconnect with them. I'm too different. Being in Didja has sorted me out so much that I'm normal and the rest of them are all quite off their rockers.'

'What has brought you to this conclusion, Einstein?'

'They're not mad at me.'

Iris blinked slowly, letting his words sink in. 'Wait a second. Let me get this straight. You left home two years ago.' He nodded. 'You come back, welcomed warmly into the bosom of your family, and you're upset because they're not angry?'

'You've summed it up beautifully.' That was just like her. She cut straight to the chase, to the heart of the problem. He'd seen her do it time and time again with her little patients. He'd also seen her handle the parents of her patients equally adeptly.

'Why do you think they should be mad?'

'Because I hurt them.'

Iris nodded slowly. 'What if they've forgiven you?'

Dex frowned for a second as though he hadn't even thought of this possibility. 'Hmm.'

'Or perhaps it's the simple fact that you've realised your childhood wasn't a sham, it wasn't a lie. You were raised in a caring environment with people who loved you. That's special, Dex. And perhaps facing this fact makes you re-evaluate your life. That you're not the black sheep or the unwanted child you always thought you were. You were loved. *Are* loved.' She pointed to the door. 'Go. Spend more time with them.'

She needed him out, away from her right now because she was far too vulnerable to have him close and alone the way they were now. He was on the floor, no longer slumped over but lying down, head propped up on his elbow as he stared at her with those glorious brown eyes she dreamt of every night.

'I'm fine for now. I told them I was coming to check up on you.'

'You've checked. Now go.' She shifted further back on the bed, needing as much distance between them as possible.

Dex sat up and looked at her carefully. She had a look in her eyes, a deep abiding look that he could simply lose himself in. The woman was really starting to drive him quietly insane. Had she any idea just how often he thought of her? How often he wanted to hold her close? He wanted to kiss her again, to pull her hair from the bands and thread his fingers through the glorious reddish-blonde locks. He wanted to feel that hair whisper tantalisingly over his skin, knowing the long silky strands would drive him absolutely wild.

'Don't look at me like that.' The words were barely a whisper.

'I can't help it.'

'Try. We're in your parents' house.'

Dex's smile was deep and highly seductive. 'Only makes it more fun.'

'Dex! Stop saying things like that. Honestly, do you have any idea just how crazy that makes me?'

He slid to his knees and shuffled across the polished floorboards towards the bed. 'I think *you're* the one who should stop saying things like that. It only makes me want you even more when you talk like that.'

'Dex.' She held up both her hands to stop him. 'We can't. It's not right.' She looked at him and when he seemed about to protest, she went on. 'We're colleagues. That's all.'

'What about friends?'

Iris nodded slowly. 'Yes, we're friends but right now I'm far too vulnerable for anything except what I'm about to face tomorrow. I know part of the reason you came along on this journey was to see your family but you said you wanted to support me as well.'

'That's right.'

'Well, the best way you can support me is not to get all… playboyish on me.'

'Playboyish?' He raised his eyebrows.'

'You know what I mean.'

'Is that even a word?'

'Stop it. You're being cute again. Besides, I don't ever want to be another one of your conquests.'

'Iris!' It was as though she'd slapped him again. He was shocked she thought that. Had the woman no idea at all just how incredibly, how power-fully she affected him? He'd had nights when he'd had to go and sleep outside under the stars, risking the mozzies and the flies attacking him because he couldn't stand the fact that their apart-ments were so close.

He'd imagined her, far too many times, un-dressing, getting ready for bed, lying down and sleeping, her lovely long hair fanned out across the starkness of the white pillows. He'd imagined kissing her, holding her, loving her. Oh, no. She was far from being just another conquest, as she termed it. She was dangerous and she was about to become a mother. He didn't do families. He'd do well to stop flirting with her and heed her words right now and leave her in peace.

He stood, surprising Iris that she'd managed to get through to him.

'Dinner's at eight,' he said as he headed towards the door. 'Dress is casual.'

'Dex.' He stopped when she called his name, his hand on the doorknob, ready to make his get-away. 'Give your family a chance. Everything's no doubt a little overwhelming, for all of you, but after seeing you together, adoption or no adoption, there's no doubt in my mind that you *are* a family. They love you very much.'

'I know.' With that, he nodded and left her alone, staring at a blank door.

The following morning Iris was up so bright and early she thought she'd beaten the sun. There was no way she could sleep and as she seemed to be full of nervous energy, she donned some sweats and headed outside for a run. The neighbourhood where Dexter's parents lived was an older suburb with older, more classic styles of architecture. It was quaint, charming, and she really liked it.

When she returned, she showered and dressed quickly before making her way down to the kitchen. She was only looking for a glass of juice but when she walked into the room she jumped in surprise when she saw Dex sitting at the island bench, reading the newspaper.

'You scared me.' She placed her hand on her heart.

'And good morning to you, too. Been for a run?'

'Huh?'

'I thought I heard you head out earlier.'

'Yes. I needed to expel some nervous energy.' Iris took the juice from the fridge and Dex instantly handed her two glasses. She poured him some juice. 'You couldn't sleep either?'

'Far too much going on to sleep.' He smiled as he accepted the drink. He held his out to hers, ready to make a toast. 'To…good days like these.'

'The day's only begun. How can you toast to that? What if it's a really bad day?'

'It won't be. Trust me.' He clinked his glass against hers. 'I have a good feeling about this.'

'All right. I'll trust your feeling. Joss told me how you once did a rain dance so you wouldn't have to go out on house calls and that it did indeed rain. So I guess if you have a good feeling about this, I'd better trust it.'

'Thank you, Iris.' He was touched by her words. 'Thank you for believing in me.' Dex held her gaze for a long moment and Iris found herself once more mesmerised by the man she knew was all wrong for her. He was a 'fly by the seat of his pants' type of person and she liked everything to be neatly organised and planned. He thought nothing of entertaining two or three women at one time, she liked the sole attention of one man. Their worlds had run on very different courses and whilst they had converged briefly, enabling them to help and support each other, that would soon change.

She would have a baby. A child to take care of, and the thought terrified her.

These were the things she had to keep reminding herself about, especially when she was captured by that hypnotic stare of his, the one that said he'd like to gather her close and take his time exploring her mouth, her neck and the rest of the secrets her body kept.

She could feel herself beginning to melt, wanting to move closer to him, and a small sigh escaped her lips. The sound seemed to snap Dex back to reality and he broke the hold he had over her, shifting from his chair, walking over to a cupboard and pulling out a frying pan.

'Hungry? I could make you an omelette for breakfast.'

'Uh…no, thanks. I don't think I'll be eating anything this morning.' She tried not to notice his abrupt change in mood. It was as though he was drawing her closer with one of those saucy, sexy looks and then pushing her away with both hands, determined to hold her at bay. One moment she had the feeling he wanted nothing else than to spend all of his time getting to know her better…a lot better…and then it was as though he wanted to be anywhere but where she was.

'I have a few things to take care of before we head off this morning,' she said.

Dex shrugged. 'Fair enough.'

Iris finished her juice and put her glass into the dishwasher before heading to the door. She stopped there and turned back to look at Dex. 'Thanks for offering to come with me, Dex. It means a lot.'

Dex opened his mouth to reply but no words came out. In the spot where she currently stood, the sunlight was streaming in through a nearby window, encompassing her in a heavenly glow. The way her hair shone, the way her eyes sparkled, the way her words carried pure sincerity—it left him stunned. She was so incredibly beautiful both inside and out and he knew in that one moment that something very powerful was happening.

Iris wasn't just a colleague any more. She wasn't just a friend he was helping out. In that one instant she became much more and his heart rate increased with a resounding firm rhythm.

He closed his mouth and nodded, swallowing over the sudden scratchiness in his throat. With that, she left the room and he stood there, frying pan hanging limply by his side as he tried to figure out what exactly had just occurred.

CHAPTER TEN

THE meeting with Anya was to be held at the home of the foster-parents. The solicitor in charge of the case would meet her and Dex there.

Even now, as she sat in the parked car Dex had borrowed from his father, looking out at the house they were supposed to go into, Iris still wasn't sure what she was doing. Taking on a baby was a huge responsibility and not one to be entered into lightly.

What would happen when Anya grew up into a teenager? Would she be better off in Didja or would she feel isolated? Would Iris still be able to take the job in Melbourne with a baby in tow? Would Anya benefit from being raised in the city as opposed to the outback?

'How are you doing?' Dex asked as he undid his seat belt and pulled the keys from the ignition.

'Uh…' Iris breathed out slowly.

'That good, huh? Here, let me help you.' He unclipped her seat belt, took her handbag off the back seat and gave it to her. 'Time to face the music.' He turned to get out of the car but Iris clamped a hand around his elbow to stop him. Dex looked at her, seeing fear and trepidation in her eyes.

'My mind is whirring so fast…' She stopped and shrugged her shoulders. 'What am I supposed to do, Dex?'

'You're supposed to step up to the plate and do what you need to do. You also need to know that you have not only my full support but Melissa's and Joss's as well. You also have a job available to you in Didja for six months or longer, should you so choose.'

Iris studied him for a moment. 'Is that your decision or Joss's?'

'Both. At the Didja clinic, we look after our own. At the moment, you are part of that family and whatever you need is yours.'

'And you'll come in with me?' She pointed to the house. 'In there?'

'You supported me when I stood in front of my parents' door yesterday, I'm here to do the same for you.' And once it was over, he would keep his distance. He was pretty certain she would leave at the end of her contract because she already had another job lined up. Still, Joss had been hopeful that taking on the baby might prompt Iris to stay in Didja for quite a lot longer than her contract dictated.

Dex, however, was still trying to figure out what on earth had happened earlier that morning. When he'd looked at her the sensations had been incredibly powerful and he knew some people might misconstrue those to be feelings of love, but Dex knew that couldn't possibly be the case. He didn't do love. He didn't do relationships and he didn't do happy families.

He'd been abandoned at birth, put up for adoption and then lied to for thirty-one years. Whilst he had taken the first step towards healing the pain of deception his parents had inflicted, Dex knew the last thing he needed to take on was more responsibility. Babies meant responsibility and a whole lot more. If that was what Iris chose to saddle herself with, that was her decision. It would mean that in time she could legally adopt Anya and Dex knew on a personal level that he couldn't deal with that. Whatever he felt for Iris, however serious it might be, it stopped. Today.

Iris didn't move and Dex decided it was time to get this over and done with. He climbed from the car and walked around to the passenger side, opening the door for her. Iris reluctantly exited and stood on the footpath. There were two other cars in the driveway and she wondered if that meant everyone was already inside, waiting for her.

'No time like the present.' Dex linked his arm with hers and she let him. She realised she'd certainly come a long way in such a few short weeks. When she'd first met Dex, she hadn't been able to abide him touching her. Now, though, the warmth of his arm against hers was comforting. The warmth from his body was relaxing and the encouragement she saw reflected in his eyes was exactly what she needed.

He walked her to the door, then removed his arm but linked their hands. 'Big breath,' he instructed, and looked at her intently. 'You can do this, Iris. You're a strong woman.'

'I don't feel like one,' she said softly.

'Trust me on this.' He gave her hand a reassuring squeeze. 'You're strong, Iris.' Strong, intelligent and, oh, so incredibly beautiful. He'd seen her in so many ways, aloof, certain, commanding, afraid, alluring, terrified, just to name a few. Above all, though, she was a strong woman and that internal strength came from her ability to give, to be compassionate and to love. 'I know that for a fact and so should you.' He held her gaze for another moment, hoping she believed him. 'You can do this,' he reiterated, before leaning forward and tapping twice with the door knocker. A moment later, it was answered by a woman with a bright smiling face and curly black hair.

'Hi. You must be Iris. Come in.' She invited them both inside. 'I'm Tacula,' she chattered excitedly. 'And is this your husband? I hadn't realised you were married. Oh, a two-parent family would be much better for Anya to be raised in.'

Both Iris and Dex started talking at once at the misconception but Tacula seemed to wave their words away, not really listening to either of them as she beckoned them further into the house. Upstairs, they could hear the sound of little feet running around and Iris wondered how many children Tacula was presently caring for.

As they neared the kitchen, which was where everyone seemed to be gathered, she could hear the sounds of a baby whimpering and her heart turned over. She loved babies and children. She felt such empathy with them and it was the main reason she'd become a paediatrician. Having her

own—instantly having her own—was something
she most definitely hadn't planned on, though.

'Come through,' Tacula encouraged, and then
when they were standing in the doorway, she
pointed to the solicitors in the room and performed the introductions.

'And this is Iris's husband.' Tacula turned to
Dex. 'I'm sorry, I didn't catch your name.'

'Dex. Dex Crawford,' he replied. He glanced at
Iris to see whether she was going to explain the
mistake or whether he should, but he found her
staring at a small bassinet in the corner of the room,
a whimpering baby girl trying desperately to make
her presence known. He let the mistake slide. There
were more important things happening here.

Iris let go of his hand and walked slowly
towards the baby. Her heart was beating faster
and emotion was starting to well up in her throat.
Francie's baby. Francie and Nigel's little girl. All
alone. With no mum. No dad. Whimpering in a
bassinet in the corner of a strange place.

Tears started to fill Iris's eyes.

'And, of course, that's Anya, but you probably
already know that,' Tacula said brightly. 'I've
been trying to get her to settle without being
cuddled to sleep.' There was a slight warning in

the woman's voice, as though she didn't want Iris to go any closer to the baby. Iris didn't care.

She stood beside the bassinet now and looked down at the baby who'd grown so much since she'd last seen her four months ago. She looked like Francie even though her face was all red and her nose all snuffly. A tear slid silently down Iris's cheek as she reached down to pick the baby up.

'Oh, if you wouldn't mind leaving her there.' Tacula came closer to try and stop Iris. 'As I said, I'm trying to train her to…'

The woman droned on, meaning well, but Iris wasn't listening. The world around her had disappeared, all except for Dex who she could feel urging her on, urging her to do whatever it was in her heart to do.

Iris cradled the baby in her arms and her heart flooded with such pain, sympathy and love for the orphaned little girl. Anya may not have any idea what was going on, she may not know she'd never see her parents again, she may even be wondering if she'd done something wrong. The facts remained, though, she was less than a year old and she was all alone.

The tears that Iris had been unable to cry a few days ago came hard and fast now as the realisation that she would never see her friends again hit home. Grief became the dominant emotion and as she cradled the child, her heart ached.

Feeling the warmth of someone's arm around her shoulders, Iris looked, not at all surprised to see Dex standing beside her, urging her to lean into him. He held her. He supported her, offered comfort and gave her the strength she needed to cope.

'They're gone, Dex,' she sobbed. 'They're really gone and Anya's all alone.' She sniffed and he dabbed at her face with his handkerchief.

Dex looked at the little mite who had snuggled into Iris and had stopped whimpering. Anya's eyes were now closed, her nose and face blotchy and her thumb slipping into her mouth as she suckled herself to a better sleep.

She was gorgeous and he, too, felt the stirrings of empathy for her. The baby was all alone but he knew Iris would take good care of her. His colleague may not have the first idea on how to be a mother but she had an abundance of love and that in itself would be enough to get her started. Besides, if she stayed in Didja, she would have a world of support and knowledge right at her fingertips. At this thought, at the thought that Iris and Anya might, just possibly, stay longer than the initial six months, Dex's heart pounded wildly.

To have Iris close, to get to spend more time with her, to... He stopped his thoughts. He wasn't supposed to be drawing closer to her. He was supposed to be extracting himself from her life simply because she was causing far too much a disruption in his. Dex looked at Iris who was looking at Anya and that same sensation he'd experienced earlier that morning swamped him once more.

Love? Was that what he was feeling towards Iris because if it was, if it was real love and he wasn't simply deluding himself, then he really needed to put as much distance between them as possible.

After today, he rationalised, not yet willing to move away from woman and child. Today she needed him and he was going to follow through on his promise to support her. She looked so calm and relaxed at the moment and, unbeknownst to her, even more beautiful holding Anya in her arms.

Dex focused on the little girl and knew she was going to steal many hearts. Already, after a matter of mere minutes, he already had feelings for the innocent babe. Was this what his parents had felt when they'd looked down at him? A small baby boy? Abandoned by his mother? Had their hearts filled instantly with love—just as Iris's had? Had the childless couple vowed to care for him? To love him and to raise him as their own?

In some ways, Iris reminded him a lot of his own mother—a woman who soldiered on, despite whatever life threw at her. Dex dropped a kiss to Iris's head, knowing she would make a great mother. Her heart really was big and strong and she had so much to offer the orphaned baby.

Iris's tears started to subside and after blowing her nose, she bent to place a little kiss on Anya's head. She'd been about to vow to the child that she would take her in, that she would care for her, that she would love her—but something stopped her. Iris frowned and kissed Anya's head again, lingering for a moment.

'She's hot.'

Dex instantly placed a hand on Anya's forehead. 'You're right.' He turned to face Tacula. 'You said Anya's been having trouble settling? Sleeping?'

'Yes. She's been whimpering a lot during the last few nights. It's just because she's in a strange place. It happens to a lot of them when they first arrive. If she's taught the structure of a good routine, it shouldn't take long for that to stop.'

'She has a fever.' Iris was angry but she controlled her tone. She placed the child in the bassinet, not interested in any excuses. What mattered now was that Anya was sick and she was just the person to make her better.

'How long was she in Tarparnii?' Dex asked as he walked to the kitchen and started pulling open drawers until he found a clean cotton tea-towel. He soaked it in cold water and squeezed it out as the solicitors checked their notes.

'About six weeks.'

'Check her ankles and her wrists. Any signs of swelling?' Dex returned to Iris's side and now that Iris had removed most of the baby's clothing, he began to sponge the child down.

'Oedema at the ankles. Mild at the wrists.' Iris glanced at him. 'What am I looking for?'

'Yullom Cigru fever. It's quite common in Tarparnii but only in areas where there's bad sanitation. It mainly affects young children and the elderly. If Francie and Nigel were working in areas with no running water, there's a good chance Anya's picked it up.'

'Yellow what?' Tacula was asking, but neither of them paid her much heed.

'Check her tongue. Is there discolouration?' Dex kept sponging the baby. 'She'll need an IV for replacement fluids, a full course of antibiotics and most likely steroids. The disease, if left untreated for too long, can deteriorate the bronchioles. We've got to get her strong.'

Iris forced Anya's mouth open, much to the baby's chagrin. 'Discoloured.'

'Is it contagious?' The solicitor wanted to know.

'It is. You should all come to the hospital and be checked. That includes any other children in the house, Tacula. Worst-case scenario would be that you'd need a course of antibiotics so nothing major to worry about,' Dex said as he handed the wet towel to Iris. Anya was now in full crying mode but at least it proved that her lungs weren't as bad as they'd thought. 'Keep sponging her.' He snapped his phone from his waistband and called for an ambulance.

'Tacula?' Iris said over her shoulder. 'Could you please pack up all of Anya's things? I'll take them now.'

'Of course,' the woman answered immediately, a hint of contrition in her tone.

Iris looked down at the sick baby but all she saw was a tiny girl in need of a whole lot of love. Thankfully, she had a whole lot of love to give.

'We'll get things in order and get back to you,'

one of the solicitors said as they started to pack up the papers on the table.

'Iris can sign whatever papers she needs to at the hospital.' Dex closed his phone and looked at the adults in the room. 'Which is where I expect to see you all in less than half an hour. Tell the triage nurse that you're specifically there to see me.'

'You can do that?' Iris asked quietly as she kept sponging Anya down.

'I used to work there. I can still pull a few strings when I have to.'

She smiled and sighed with relief as she met his gaze for a moment. He was such a wonderful man. How could she ever have thought him selfish and self-centred? Iris couldn't help herself and leaned over to kissed his cheek. 'Thank you, Dex. You're fantastic.'

When she looked at him like that, Dex felt his gut tighten. Those same love-like sensations washed over him and he wondered how he was supposed to keep his distance. How was he supposed to treat her as an indifferent colleague, to not hold her and smother her body with kisses? It was impossible because every time she looked at him as she was doing now, he wanted to haul her close and never, ever let her go!

He nodded briskly, accepting her compliment before moving away from her. 'I'll go pack Anya's things into the car. Keep an eye on her.'

Iris was a little puzzled at his abrupt change in mood. One second he was being so sweet, kind and thoughtful and the next—it was as though he had to turn and run away as fast as he could. He hadn't accidentally touched her scars, which she was still sure repulsed him. In fact, he hadn't touched her at all.

But she had touched him. She'd leaned over and kissed him but she'd meant it in the spirit of friendship and—

Her thoughts were cut short as Anya started to shake, her little body convulsing.

'Get me a bottle of cold water,' she said over her shoulder.

'Who, me?' one of the solicitors asked.

'Yes. There should be baby bottles somewhere on the bench. She needs water now.' Iris checked her watch, noting the time as she made sure that Anya couldn't hit or kick anything or bite her tongue.

'Maybe we should wait for the other guy to come back. He seems to know what he's talking about.' The solicitor spoke from the bench but when Iris turned to glare at him, it was to find that he was pouring cold filtered water into a bottle.

'*I'm* the paediatrician. If there's anyone qualified to look after Anya, it's me. Dex is an accident and emergency specialist.' And she was thankful he'd been to Tarparnii and had been able to diagnose Anya's condition so quickly. Of course, once they had the baby at the hospital and stabilised, they could run further tests. Iris had planned on staying in Perth for a few days but she'd never have guessed she'd be spending them in a hospital.

Accepting the bottle, Iris tested it first and checked her watch. Ten seconds. Anya had only been like this for ten seconds and yet it felt like an eternity. Was this what motherhood was going to be like? Such jerky and intense emotions, being switched on and off like a tap? The baby's crying began again in earnest. Iris instantly picked the frightened baby up and put the bottle teat into her mouth.

'There you go, sweetest one. Shh. It's all right. I'm here.'

Anya drank greedily and Iris realised she was more dehydrated than she'd originally surmised.

'Slowly. Slowly,' she crooned as she walked

with Anya in her arms over to a chair and sat down. She held out the wet towel to the solicitor and asked him to wet it again.

'She will be all right, won't she?' the solicitor asked, watching in alarm as he squeezed out the cloth.

'Of course.' Iris spoke to the baby rather than anyone else. 'Adorable Anya is going to be just fine and grow up to be as wonderful as her mother.'

Dex heard Iris's words as he walked back into the kitchen and at the sight of Iris sitting there, talking calmly to the baby who was sucking down the cold water rather quickly, the tightening in his gut instantly returned. He'd managed to quickly get himself under control whilst he'd performed the menial task of packing the car. So much stuff for such a young baby. Then again, he rationalised, Anya was female and it must be that X chromosome that inspired the need to have too many clothes and to need way too much stuff.

However, the two of them together, woman and child, certainly made a wonderful sight. It was the prettiest picture he could ever remember seeing and he pulled out his phone and snapped a photograph. He knew he'd no doubt torture himself with that very image once both Iris and Anya were out of his life. Oh, yes, the fact that Iris was a very special lady wasn't a fact that escaped him at all.

Iris looked up then and saw him standing there so he walked forward, putting his phone back into his pocket. 'How is she?'

'She had a convulsion. Eleven seconds.'

'Felt like an eternity?' he asked as he came closer but not too close. Keeping his distance was paramount if he was going to control his rising libido. The attraction he felt for Iris certainly intensified with each moment he was in her company.

'Right, that's it for us,' the solicitor said. 'We'll see you at the hospital.' With that, they high-tailed it out of there as fast as possible. The next moment he and Iris were alone in a stranger's kitchen.

'So…' Dex pointed to Anya 'She's at least keeping the fluids down.'

'I can't tell if they're really doing any good yet. Her body hasn't rejected the water so that's a good thing. I just wish I had a thermometer and the IV line and everything I need to treat her properly.' Her frustration was evident.

'She'll do fine and so will you.'

'You sound so certain.' Iris raised her eyes to meet his gaze.

Dex nodded slowly. 'You have love to give, Iris.

She needs love.' As he said the words, a picture that hung on the wall of his parents' house came to mind of his mother, at a similar age to Iris, holding him as a baby in her arms, no doubt thinking the same sort of thing.

'Can it be that simple?'

'Yes. It can.' He nodded. 'It was for my parents. Throughout my entire childhood, my adolescence, my medical school days—everything—my parents were there for me. Helping me, caring for me, loving me.'

'They were only trying to protect you, Dex. I mean, when they didn't tell you about the adoption.'

'I know.' He shrugged as though he didn't care but the tone of his voice told her otherwise. 'But it hurt. I trusted them and they deceived me. I understood their reasons but that wasn't the point. They lied and that's what hurt the most. Painfully so.'

'That's understandable but what about now? How does it feel now that you've seen them again? Has time managed to heal your wounds?' She'd been wanting to ask him and was pleased an opportunity had finally turned up.

He gave her one of those gorgeous half-smiles. 'Things are better than I'd anticipated.' And even more so because he'd had her unwavering support throughout it all. She was quite a woman. He'd known she was strong—she had to be to have lived through what she had. Now, though, he was getting to see at first hand just how incredible Iris Tennant really was and the more he saw, the more he— Dex stopped his thoughts immediately and looked away from her, shoving his hands into his pockets.

Iris watched him, watched the shift in him, and wondered what he'd been thinking. It was as though she could see the mask coming down into place, keeping him safe from everyone around him in case someone else he trusted hurt him again. She wanted to let him know that that didn't have to be the case, that he didn't need to wear a mask. All he had to do was to be his true self, in all situations.

But who was she to talk? She'd worn a mask for the past few years, cutting people out of her life and focusing on work. She'd always known what she'd wanted from life. A good job in a flourishing hospital. To meet a man and fall in love. To marry that man. To buy a house. To one day have children. To live happily ever after.

It hadn't happened that way at all and after two short years of marriage she'd been left a physically and emotionally scarred widow who wasn't at all sure what she was supposed to do next. She'd recovered and she'd done it by hiding much of herself away from others. She'd also made sure that she'd relied on no one for support. That's the way it had been…until she'd met Dex.

He'd witnessed her during some very dark moments and he'd been wonderful. He'd been supportive and in turn she'd wanted to support him. Whilst there was still a very strong pull towards him, a very strong desire to have his mouth on hers again and again and again, Iris also knew that in coming to Perth, in supporting each other, in letting the other person have a glimpse of that inner vulnerability, it was also pulling them apart.

Iris was about to take on the full-time care of a small baby. That would mean a lot of work and a lot of change. She had no idea how she was going to work full time at the children's hospital in Melbourne and decided at this stage not to think about it…which was unlike her. She wasn't a moment-to-moment type of person. She looked at Dex, standing there looking utterly adorable with his hands shoved into his pockets, his eyes on the baby in her arms. *He* was definitely the fly by the seat of his pants type of guy and perhaps spending a bit more time with him had made that quality rub off on her.

Anya finished the bottle and Iris shifted the baby up onto her shoulder and started to gently rub her back. She breathed in that yummy baby smell and sighed.

'You look good together.'

Iris looked at Dex and smiled. 'It feels so right. So natural. I never thought it could feel like this.'

'I guess Francie knew what she was doing when she asked you to be guardian.'

Iris nodded slowly. 'I guess she did.' She stared at him, their eyes meeting and melding, both of them feeling that strong tug of desire whilst at the same time trying to draw as far away from it as possible. When he looked at her like that, she started to lose control of all rational thought and all she wanted him to do now was to come and hold her in his arms. To be there for her. To support her, not just for now but for ever.

He swallowed, his Adam's apple moving up and down, and he shoved his hands further into his pockets as though needing them there to stop him from reaching for her. If that was indeed the case, it made Iris feel very special. Then again, making women feel special was his speciality.

His charm, his charisma, his chivalry. He knew how to romance a woman. He seemed to know instinctively what to say, how to offer support, what to do to make a woman feel as though she was the only one in the world and he could look at her all day long.

She knew he wasn't reliable when it came to affairs of the heart. She knew he had his own issues to deal with. She knew they were colleagues for only a few more months and then she'd leave. She knew if he ever saw the scars on her body that they would drive him far, far away. She knew he was all wrong for her, wasn't even her type, and yet, as he stood there before her, his brown eyes so incredibly intense, Iris had the feeling that she was completely in love with him.

The knowledge shocked her to her core.

She looked away, wanting to shout the word 'No' at the top of her lungs. That couldn't be right. She couldn't be in love with Dex. He was so wrong for her. He was a playboy. He wasn't fatherhood material.

Reason after reason came to mind and yet none of them seemed able to shift the fact that she was indeed in love with him.

Tacula came in, announcing the ambulance had

arrived, and Iris was glad of the diversion. As though in a daze, and making sure she kept as far away from Dex as possible, Iris went through the motions of providing care for little Anya.

Anya was her responsibility now and it helped her to realise there was no room in her life for any man. Dex was a colleague and that was all. Yes, they'd shared some incredibly personal moments since she'd first arrived in Didja but nothing more could come of it.

She needed to focus solely on the next few months, to figure out where her new life was going to lead her, and it was a life which didn't include Dexter Crawford.

CHAPTER ELEVEN

ANYA stayed in hospital for three days before everyone was satisfied.

'Ordinarily, we'd like her to stay the entire week to monitor her more closely,' the attending paediatrician had said. 'But given that she's going back to Didja, where she'll be surrounded by doctors and nurses, I don't see why she can't go home.'

Thankfully, Tacula, the children she looked after and the solicitors had all tested negative for Yullom Cigru, as had both she and Dex. At least containment had been maintained.

As Iris paced around her apartment in Didja, she thought of how wonderfully supportive Dex had been. He'd spent time at the hospital pulling whatever strings he'd needed to, making sure Anya received the best possible care. He'd been treated as the prodigal son returning home by his colleagues and many people—most of them female—had come to the infants' nursery in order to catch up with Dex.

The Crawfords had also been supportive, Ruth giving Iris lots of tips and tricks for dealing with instant parenthood. The longer they'd stayed in Perth, the more Dex had relaxed around his family, realising that they had indeed forgiven and forgotten the past. They were quite an amazing family and by the time Iris and Dex left to head back to Didja, all of the Crawfords were planning to attend Joss and Melissa's up-and-coming wedding.

'And we're looking forward to seeing you, too, and little Anya.' Ruth had hugged Iris just as tight. 'You call me at any time, day or night, if you're not sure what to do or you just need to chat or anything. Understand?'

Iris had smiled and nodded. Anya coming into her life had changed everything dramatically. Where she had been more than happy to keep herself aloof and impersonal with almost everyone she met, she was now finding it impossible. For a start, when they arrived back in Didja, baby in tow, the town put on such a welcome-home party Iris was almost moved to tears at their support and generosity. Joss even insisted that Iris take another week off to settle Anya into her new life.

'I can't believe everyone has gone to so much trouble,' she confided to Melissa the next day. 'Everyone's been so helpful. I've received lots of home-made baby food so I don't need to feed her that store stuff.'

'That'll be Minerva's doing. She's a stickler for home-made food.'

'And people have been dropping in gifts, clothes, toys. I even had Mr Bloffwith present me with a hand-crafted crib for Anya. It wasn't second-hand or anything like that. He'd *made* it just for Anya.' Iris was still astounded at people's generosity.

Melissa laughed and hugged her friend close. 'Welcome to Didja, Iris. It's their way of making sure Anya is happy, but I have to say I know exactly how you feel. They're an overwhelming bunch but everything is done with the utmost love.'

'And Bub has insisted that when I start work next week, to leave Anya with her at the hospital. She said I could enrol the baby in the town's day-care facility only when she was completely satisfied the Yullom Cigru fever was definitely out of Anya's system.'

Melissa chortled at this. 'Bub's just saying that because she wants Anya all to herself. You just watch. It'll be months before she'll deem Anya well enough to go into day care.'

And she was right. Iris had just finished her first full week of being a working mother and whilst it had been different, it hadn't been as crazy as she'd thought it might be. 'And that's because you're getting lots of help,' she told herself as she went to check on Anya.

The baby was sleeping peacefully in her hand-made crib, wearing a blue and yellow polka-dot hand-made dress, a hand-made mobile of soft-toy Australian animals hung over her and her wall was covered with hand-made pictures from Didja's pre-school children, who had wanted to welcome Anya to their town.

Many people came to town with their children, moving there for work or other reasons, yet little orphaned Anya seemed to have been adopted not just by Iris but by the entire town, and she began to wonder how on earth she was supposed to leave here in four months' time.

Staying in Didja made a lot of sense on so many levels. Joss, of course, had offered her a job for life, pointing out the benefits of raising a child in a small caring community as opposed to a large city like Melbourne. Then there was Melissa, such a close friend whom Iris would love to stay close to. Bub, Minerva, Areva and even Stig had become good friends with her as well as many others within the town.

And then there was Dex.

Iris sighed as she walked out of Anya's room and sat down on the lounge. She picked up the television remote and flicked through the small array of channels before switching it off, knowing her mind wouldn't settle.

Since they'd arrived back in Didja, Dex seemed to be the only member of the town who was keeping his distance. He was polite and professional when they were in clinic together and if he saw her in the street, he'd stop, say hello and ask her questions about Anya's health. That was it. No pick-up lines. No invitations out to dinner. No marriage proposals.

She was a single mother now and as such had fallen off his radar as an interesting target. It shouldn't hurt. It was what she wanted as well. There could never be anything but professional courtesy between herself and Dex because even the thought of a happily ever after ending only brought a lump to her throat and a fresh wave of tears.

She still loved him. There was no doubt about that. Whenever she saw him, her heart would flip-flop with delight like an adolescent schoolgirl seeing the boy she liked so much across a crowded classroom. His earthy scent almost drove her to distraction at times but she was learning to cope with that.

He alone was the reason that she was still considering Melbourne. Taking the job in the city hospital would mean extremely long hours, and whilst that hadn't been a problem before, it was certainly a problem now. So she'd contacted the hospital and informed them she would be unable to take the position. Now she was looking around for part-time jobs, not caring if she consulted privately or at a hospital just so long as she was able to spend a lot of time with Anya.

Iris shook her head, knowing the answer was right in front of her, knowing the best thing would be to stay here, but she couldn't. She couldn't stay so close to Dex and not be able to be with him. She accepted the facts and knew she needed to move on, to move forward, both for herself and for Anya. Dex had his life here in Didja and as she'd been the one to enter his world, it was only right that she leave it and find where she fitted best.

'But I like it here,' she whispered into the dark.

* * *

Dex was about to head out of his consulting room to make himself a quick cuppa before the next patient arrived when he heard Iris out in the corridor. He removed his hand from the doorknob, walked back to his chair and sat down. He'd wait a bit longer.

Usually, he didn't go out of his way to completely avoid her but when he was able to do it, it simply made it easier rather than having to make polite small talk. It was what both of them had automatically done on their return from Perth. Circumstances had changed and that was all there was to it.

He knew Iris was busy and he wanted to give her the space she needed. She was now trying to juggle motherhood and work and whilst he knew the people of Didja had rallied around her in true outback fashion, it would still be a lot for her to cope with.

However, there were so many times during his evenings alone in his apartment that he'd wanted to go next door, to sit and chat with her. To find out how she was coping, whether or not she needed any help. He'd half hoped she'd go and sit in the courtyard of an evening once Anya was asleep and just sit and enjoy a quiet glass of wine.

That maybe if she did, she'd allow him to join her. None of it had happened.

He'd found himself going to the pub less often than before but when he was there, he would see the same people, break up the same fights—usually between Carto and Bluey—but it just didn't have the same relaxing buzz it once had. Joss and Melissa had given him a clean bill of health with regard to the accident he'd been involved in at the beginning of the year and tomorrow he'd even volunteered to head out on house calls.

Joss's head nearly exploded he was so shocked at the offer.

'What's the catch?' his friend asked.

'There's no catch. I need to step up and accept responsibility.'

'But you hate house calls.'

'So? I have to do a lot of things I don't like.' Such as co-existing with the woman he was in love with. Dex pushed the thought away.

'But you *hate* house calls,' Joss reiterated, stupefied to hear those words coming from his friend's mouth.

'Look at it this way. Perhaps I didn't like doing house calls before because I was always walking into happy family situations. Homes where parents didn't necessarily lie to their children.'

Joss nodded. 'Lis thought it was something like that.'

'My big sister been psychoanalysing me again?' Dex asked, raising an amused eyebrow.

Joss grinned. 'She does that.'

'Well, now that I've reconciled with my parents, maybe it's now fine for me to see people in those situations and not be upset by them.'

'Or perhaps you want to avoid being around Iris all day long and that way you don't have to play your little games.'

'What?' Dex looked at him as though he'd grown an extra head. 'I don't know what you're on about, mate.'

Joss merely shook his head. 'Ever since you returned from Perth, you haven't been the same Dex we all know and love.'

'Well, sor-ry.'

'That's not a criticism.'

'Sounded like one.'

'It wasn't. It's just you haven't been going to the pub as much as usual.'

'I was there the last three nights in a row,' Dex felt compelled to point out.

'And you sat and talked to Nev and Kev three nights straight.'

'So?'

'Dex, you didn't try to chat to a single woman, blonde, brunette or otherwise.'

'And that means I've changed?'

'It means something *inside* you has changed. Maybe it's being reunited with your family or maybe it's...'

'What?' Dex raised his chin as though not afraid to hear what Joss had to say. 'Go on. Tell me.'

'Perhaps it's Iris.'

Dex snorted a laugh. 'Again with blaming Iris for a change in me.'

'I'm not *blaming* Iris, I'm merely pointing out that you're acting differently and Lis and I think it's because of the way you feel about her.'

'And what way is that?' Dex was really starting to get angry now. Joss may be his best friend, he may be his business partner and he may be about to become his brother-in-law, but that didn't give him any right to poke around in his love life.

'Why don't you tell me?'

Dex stared at Joss, glared at Joss, shot visual daggers at Joss for even asking such a question, but a few seconds later Dex slumped down into his chair, the fight going out of him. 'I'm confused.'

'Good.'

'Good? How is that good?'

Joss merely smiled. 'It just is.'

'How?' Dex raked a hand through his hair. 'The woman has me completely confused. I don't know which way is up. And then there's Anya and I don't want to intrude because Iris has to find her own rhythm with this motherhood thing and I'm not sleeping at night and—' He stopped and took a breath. 'And I…'

'Come on,' Joss urged eagerly. 'You what?'

'I…' Dex closed his eyes and shook his head. 'I…'

'Just say it.' Joss stood and slammed his fist on his desk.

'I love her. All right?'

Joss's grin was enormous as he came around the desk and gave Dex a brotherly hug. 'I knew it. Welcome to the club, mate.'

Dex looked at his friend and then started pacing the room. 'How can you cope? How *did* you cope? I mean, you feel this way about Lis and that's good because you two are so perfect for each other, but Iris and I…mate, we're a wrong fit.'

'How?' Joss returned to his desk and sat down.

'We're just… She has Anya to think of.'

'You're as crazy about that little girl as the rest of the town. I've seen you at the hospital, holding Anya and giving her a bottle. You're as smitten with her as you are with Iris—but in a completely different way,' Joss pointed out.

'It's just that Iris deserves…well, better than me.'

Joss's answer was to raise an eyebrow. 'And why is that?'

'You know why. I'm no good at relationships.'

'And that is based on what? Catherine? She was a floozy, Dex. She wasn't right for you and because of things she said over a decade ago, you're going to destroy your chance at happiness?'

'But I let myself love her and look how it turned out.'

'Did you *really* love her? The same way you love Iris?'

Dex thought for a moment before shaking his head. 'I just don't think I'm capable of providing a stable environment, of being firm in the commitment.'

'Why?'

'Because…well, because I've thought that for a while. Being adopted, Joss, it's like I don't know who I am any more. What if I'm like my biological father? Lis said he was a bit of a womaniser. That sounds like me.'

'He was a charmer,' Joss corrected.

'He still left our mother alone with Lis and me. He left her alone and then he died.'

'He took a job driving a truck to make some money and died in a crash!' Joss rolled his eyes. 'Stop twisting the facts.'

'Ah…but are they? I've only got Melissa's word for it and she's only got the testimony of our biological mother, who was on her deathbed at the time. The fact remains that I really don't have a clue who I am.'

'Yes, you do. You're the son of Ruth and Dwayne Crawford. You're big brother to Xandi and Mason. You're little brother to Melissa. You're my best friend. You're a pillar in this community and you're in love with Iris.'

'All right. Well, let's say things did work out right with Iris, what about Anya? She'll probably adopt Anya at some stage.'

'And you don't think you can deal with being a parent to an adopted child?'

'I don't know.' Dex shook his head.

'The situation is—'

'Different. I know. I know all that but still…'
He trailed off and shook his head. 'What if I let
Iris down? Let them both down? Am I strong
enough?' He looked at his friend again. 'I told
you I was confused.'

Joss nodded. 'Fair enough. Right then, confused man, we'll talk more later and see if you've
come up with any answers. Now, though, I have
work to do and so do you. House calls for you this
week is a definite. I'm sure you'll enjoy it—oh,
and no rain dances.' Joss had chuckled at his own
joke.

Even now, Dex shook his head and closed his
eyes at the memory of the conversation. Joss knew
him so well and could read him like a book.
Thankfully, the feeling was mutual and when Joss
had been in no-man's land over his feelings for
Melissa, Dex had been able to see through all the
ruses. Now Joss was a very happy man, about to
marry Melissa. It was fantastic to see not only his
friend but his sister that happy, and Dex was looking
forward to being best man at their wedding.

The only problem was, Iris was maid of honour
and the two of them would have to spend most of
the day together, grinning and smiling and pretending that nothing had ever happened between

them. He'd have to pretend that he wasn't in love with Iris and make sure that he kept his distance until he absolutely had to be around her. It was paramount for his own self-preservation.

He also had the new experience of his parents and siblings coming to town for the wedding. Whilst things were good between them, it was all still new and Dex was starting to feel as though his world was closing in—on all sides. Without Iris there to support him, he wasn't sure he was going to cope.

Dex knew all he had to do was to ask her to help him through and she'd do it. She was that kind of person. So caring. So giving. Even though she tried to be standoffish, he knew the real Iris. He'd seen her at some very raw moments, just as she'd witnessed a few of his. He missed her. Missed talking to her. Missed sparring with her. Missed…her smile.

He heard her laugh, through the walls of the consulting rooms, the tinkling sound making music in his ears. She had the best laugh and it was great to hear her so happy. She deserved all the happiness which came her way. Unfortunately, Dex knew, for sanity's sake, it couldn't come from him.

Iris still hadn't made a decision whether she was planning on stay on in Didja after her six-month contract. If she did, Dex realised he wouldn't be able to stand being around her day in, day out with no end in sight. At least now he knew, come the middle of the year, she would leave. He only had to hold on until then and once she'd gone, taking Anya with her, his life would slowly be able to return to normal.

Although he knew it wouldn't. He knew he'd be in love with Iris for ever but hopefully with half a country between them, the feelings would be easier to deal with.

What if she *did* decide to stay in Didja? To stay in the outback and raise her daughter? Surely it would be a better life for Anya as well as Iris with the close community support. There was no way Melbourne could offer that. If she did decide to stay, though, he wouldn't be able to function. That he knew as a certainty.

It only left him with one option. If Iris stayed, he would have to leave.

It had been two and a half weeks since they'd returned from Perth and Melissa and Joss's wedding was at the end of next week. There was so much to do, especially as she was the maid of honour. As such, it was her responsibility to organise the bachelorette party and Iris had no clue how to do this.

'What are bachelorette parties like out here in the outback?' she asked Bub after clinic was finished. Iris had come to collect Anya who had just woken from her afternoon nap.

'Much the same as the ones in the city,' Bub answered. 'You were married once. Didn't you have a party beforehand?'

Iris thought back. 'Not really. I guess a few of us girls went out to dinner.'

'Well…that's a start.'

'OK. So dinner, but where?' Iris smiled down at the little girl who had well and truly taken her heart. Anya, bless her, smiled back and held out her arms, indicating she wanted to be picked up. Iris willingly obliged, snuggling the baby close.

'How about Stiggie's?' Bub suggested.

'Yes. Good. No! Aren't the boys going there for Joss's bachelor party?'

'They're going to the pub.'

'But that's just around the corner from Stiggie's. We can't have Joss and Lis fraternising on the night. Can we?'

Bub merely chuckled. 'Well, then, darl, I'd say you have your work cut out for you.'

'Thanks. You've been no help at all.' Iris bent to pick up Anya's baby bag, which had been a gift from Bub herself. 'How was Anya today? No problems?'

'None whatsoever.' Bub caressed the baby's downy head. 'I love having her here. She's a good girl.'

'Yes, she is.' Iris kissed Anya's head. 'Addictive, too.' She transferred Anya to her hip and then picked up her briefcase. 'Well, we'd best get off. Madam here likes to eat not too soon after she wakes up.'

'Don't I know it,' Bub said. 'Oh, and you might want to ask Dex what he's got planned for Joss's party. That way, the two of you can co-ordinate your schedules.'

At the mention of Dex's name, Iris tried to ignore the way her mouth went dry and her knees went weak. She needed to stop doing that, to stop being affected by the mere mention of him. He'd made things pretty clear that now she was a single mother, he had no interest in her at all.

'Good idea,' she said, knowing she needed to say something but not wanting to end up playing twenty questions with Bub as to why she probably wasn't going to take her up on the suggestion. 'See you tomorrow. Wave byebye, Anya.' She picked up the little girl's hand and waved it up and down, Anya giggling at the action.

Iris walked out of the hospital and headed to her apartment. 'Oh, this commute is just too tough for words,' she remarked to Anya a moment later as she put her briefcase down to unlock her apartment door.

'I know what you mean. Some days the thought of walking a whole fifty steps from work to home can really add a lot of stress to your day,' Dex's rich, warm voice said from behind her, and she spun around so quickly the baby bag dropped off her shoulder. 'Let me help you with that.' Within two steps he was by her side and had lifted the strap off her arm and slung the bag onto his own shoulder.

'Er…thanks.' Her eyes devoured him. He looked so good. If she'd thought the mere mention of his name made her mouth go dry and her knees go weak, it was nothing compared to the sensations when he was standing close to her. And that scent of his. It was perfect. Wonderful. Hypnotic.

Anya wriggled on her hip and Iris looked away, belatedly realising she'd been staring at him. 'I'd best get Missy here something to eat. She gets hungry when she—'

'Wakes up after her afternoon sleep. I know.'

'You do?' Iris's eyebrows nearly hit her hairline. How on earth did he know that? He'd been treating her as persona non grata and it had hurt. How could he know anything about her or Anya?

Dex shrugged and held open the door to Iris's apartment, indicating she should go before him. 'I've dropped in a few times to see her at the hospital.' More than a few, he amended silently. 'Usually nearer the end of the day.' Or at any time he could get. To say that Anya had secured a place in his heart would be an understatement. That little miss had him wrapped right around her little finger and as she smiled her toothy smile at him now, he knew that wasn't about to change. It was insane to think such a small little thing had so much power. Perhaps it was the fact that she'd been left all alone that he empathised with. Perhaps it was the fact that she wouldn't be raised by her biological parents. Perhaps it was the fact that spending time with Anya had made him feel closer to Iris.

'Oh. I didn't know.' She picked up her briefcase and walked past him, being careful not to touch him in any way.

'Is that a problem?' He followed her in and placed the baby bag on a chair.

'No. No. Of course not. She seems to have been adopted by the entire town. They all love her.'

'Here.' He held out his hands to Anya. 'Let me hold her while you get some mushy food organised.' To Iris's chagrin, Anya leaned towards him, going willingly into his arms. If she knew Dex that well, how much time had he spent with her? Maybe more than he'd confessed. She didn't blame him. Anya was definitely an adorable baby and so easy to love, yet if he had been spending time visiting her, it only made it even clearer that he wanted nothing much to do with herself. Anya—yes. Iris—no.

Deciding not to think about it whilst he was there, Iris went to work in the kitchen, puréeing pumpkin and mixing in some rice cereal. When she came out, Dex had Anya in her high-chair, making her giggle by playing peek-a-boo. She stood there for a moment, watching the two of them, her heart turning over at seeing just how wonderful he was with the baby. He would make an incredible father.

She cut that thought off. 'Here we go. Did you want to feed her?'

'Love to,' Dex replied, and accepted the bowl of food from Iris.

Feeling a little stunned at his reply, Iris quickly recovered. 'OK, then. I'll get her bath ready. Oh, and watch—' She cut herself off in the middle of the sentence, deciding not to warn Dex about Anya's latest party trick, which was blowing rasp-berries with her tongue—usually when she had a full mouthful of food.

'Watch what?'

Iris turned and waved her words away. 'Never mind. Won't be long.' She ran the bath, laid out clean clothes and nappy and turned down Anya's crib. Usually, Anya would eat, have a bath, play with her toys, spend some time in the baby en-tertainer—a gift from the Etherington family— and then be ready for her night-time bottle. By eight-thirty the baby was usually in bed and thankfully slept all the way through until five o'clock in the morning.

'Hey!' She heard Dex call, and then, 'Anya!' His warm laughter filled the air. 'You little minx.'

Iris wetted a facecloth and headed out. 'Hey, Iris. Do you have a—' He stopped when she handed him the wet towel. 'Ah…how did you know?'

Iris shrugged.

'You could have warned me,' he said through a broad grin.

'And where would the fun have been in that? Is she all done?'

'Gobbled the lot up.'

'Good girl.' Iris took her from the high-chair and carried her through to the change table. She'd half expected Dex to leave at any moment but he stayed right through Anya's bath. Whilst Iris dressed the baby again and then put her down on the play mat, Dex went off to the kitchen to make them both a cup of tea.

Iris felt jittery having him here in her apartment, which was silly in a way because it wasn't the first time he'd been in here. It was, however, the first time he'd been this close to her since they'd got back from Perth, and now that she'd accepted her true feelings for him, it was definitely more difficult to ignore the way his closeness made her feel.

'Here you go,' he said, coming back into the room and handing her a cup of tea. 'Time to sit and relax for a few minutes.'

'Thanks.' Iris made sure she was sitting in the armchair and not on the sofa. Being too close to Dex would be a recipe for disaster. Even sitting in the same room with him was causing her heart rate to increase and her body to turn to a boneless mass of tingles. How could he have such an effect on her?

'I was wondering if we could chat about the pre-wedding parties we're supposed to be organising for the bride and groom,' he said.

'Oh, yes. Good idea.' At least now she didn't have to seek him out to do it. 'What do you have planned for Joss? I think it might be best if we don't overlap…unless overlapping parties are what happens on a regular basis in Didja.' She shrugged her shoulders. 'I really don't have a clue.'

Dex grinned, his fantastic grin, and Iris was glad she was sitting down. 'Haven't had much cause to plan bachelorette parties before?'

'Not really.' She smiled, unable to resist his charm. 'I guess I don't want to offend anyone by not inviting them.'

'Oh, that part is easily taken care of.'

'Really? How?'

'Put an add in the *Didja Gazette*.'

'What?'

'Yep. That's what I'm doing with Joss. Inviting everyone!'

'But if you invite every male and I invite every female, then it's going to be a certainty that we'll all end up at the same place.'

Dex nodded. 'The Didja pub. The centre of town. The hub of all hubs.'

Iris sighed, then slowly shook her head. 'I have no idea what I'm doing. Their wedding is at the end of next week. The parties are supposed to be this coming weekend.' The pressure of everything was starting to get to her and she was having a difficult time stopping it all from overflowing. 'Between organising this party, dress fittings, patients, house calls, Anya, dealing with my grief, wedding re-hearsals, you…' Her voice broke and she sucked in a breath. 'I feel as though I'm falling apart at the seams. Life never used to be this difficult. I was in control. I had it all worked out and now…'

Dex watched as she tried to hold back the tears, his heart aching for the woman before him. She really had been through the wringer lately but he'd had no idea just how badly it had all been affecting her. 'I thought you were coping. I mean, you looked to be coping with everything like some sort of super-mum.'

'Well, I'm not.' Iris stood and carried her cup into the kitchen, tossing the tea down the sink. She couldn't believe she was falling apart in front of Dex *again*! What was it about the man that made her spill everything out?

'Iris?'

She hadn't heard him move and gripped the edge of the bench, not wanting to turn and look at him. Those gorgeous eyes of his, the way his hair would fall at messy angles, which only enhanced his good looks, those strong supportive arms... No. She wasn't strong enough to resist him at the moment and she didn't want to be one of those women who threw themselves at men who didn't want them.

'I'm sorry if I upset you.'

'I think it's best if you just go, Dex.'

'I don't. Let me help, Iris. Let me into that world of yours where you don't let anyone.'

'I did let you in,' she said softly. 'And you hurt me.'

Dex's eyes widened at that and his heart cramped. 'I've hurt you?'

CHAPTER TWELVE

THERE was such confusion, such anguish in those three brief words that Iris turned and looked at him. Was he playing a game? Was he trying to let her down more easily? Was he lying to her?

'How? How have I hurt you?' He desperately wanted to know because he'd been doing his utmost to keep his distance so he didn't cause her any hurt. Now she was telling him otherwise?

'You shut me out of your life, Dex. When we went to Perth, I thought we'd…you know…moved onto a different level of…friendship.'

'Relationship, you mean.'

'Well, yes. All right. Friendships *are* relationships but you know what I mean. Things became more intense as we helped each other through those crazy days. You were there for me, standing by Anya's bedside in the hospital, barking orders, making everyone jump to your tune, and I thought you'd done all that because you cared…cared for Anya and…and for…me.'

Dex raked a hand through his hair. 'I do. I do care, Iris. Far too much.'

'And so you've stayed away?' Her look was one of total confusion. 'We arrived back from Perth and it was as though you cut us right off. I'd helped you through your tough time, you'd helped me through mine. Job done. See you later.' Iris paced a little as she spoke, knowing if she just stood there looking at him, she wouldn't be able to get these words out.

'At the very least, Dex, our friendship became a lot stronger.'

'It did.' The words were said softly. 'But when we got back, you didn't need my help. You had everyone in town helping you.' And he'd needed to keep his distance because she was far too appealing.

'So you just…what? Decided that as you thought you were incapable of having a lasting relationship, that you'd somehow screw it up, which is ridiculous, by the way, that you'd just push me aside?'

'Iris, it's not as cut and dried as that.'

'No? You know, when Tim first died, I was in

hospital, I was in pain…' She looked down at the floor, unable to meet Dex's gaze. 'Disfigured, and all I could feel was guilt. As I recovered, the guilt remained but I managed to push it to the back. I needed to get on with my life because that's what people do in tragic situations. You go on living.' She looked at him now. 'So that's what I did. I lived but because I hadn't dealt with the guilt, I became…lost. For the past few years I've been wandering around in a sea of confusion, trying to figure out where my life was. What was I supposed to be doing? The fact that I lived through that horrific night should mean I still have work here to do on earth, or something like that. I didn't die so I thought surely there must be a reason for that.'

'And now you have Anya. A good reason to have lived, wouldn't you say?'

'Well, there is that…but I don't know if that's all. I'm not meaning to sound morbid here but had I died, Francie would have chosen a different guardian for Anya. Don't get me wrong. Anya is an incredibly important part of my life and I love her very much. I've already put the paperwork in place to officially adopt her. I want her with me, always. And, yes…' She held out a hand to him.

'I will be telling Anya right from the beginning that she is adopted. I'll be telling her about her wonderful parents and all the good work they did throughout their lives.'

Dex nodded. 'Good. That's the way it should be. I was so mad when I found out that I was adopted. I think because I'd always known, somewhere, deep down inside, that I was…different. It wasn't that my parents treated me any differently, or loved Xandi and Mason more. It was just…I don't know…something.'

'That inner core deep down inside each of us.'

'Exactly. In the end, I guess I was more mad that they'd lied to me. After that, it made me question so many things. I had so much rage in me and if Joss hadn't encouraged me to come to Didja, goodness knows what would have happened.'

She couldn't even contemplate such a thought. 'But it didn't.'

'No. Just like you didn't die in that fire.'

'We were meant to live.' She spoke softly and her eyes met his. The heat in the room intensified as he took a step towards her.

'Meant to be here.' His gaze flicked down to look at her mouth and heat raced through her at the action. He kept moving forward, closing the distance between them. 'We were both meant to be here. Right now. In this time. At this place.' His words were deep, hypnotic. 'With each other.' He cupped her cheek and she leaned into the touch as she rested her open hands on his chest. He'd been unable to resist touching her, unable to keep his distance, to keep things platonic.

'You've come into my life, Iris. You've helped me to realise that there's more to learn, to look at the glass as though it's half-full rather than half-empty. You have been through so much and yet you go on. You have so much strength and when I'm around you, I feel the strength too. You're incredible.'

Her breathing had rapidly increased and she slid her arms up and over his shoulders as his other arm came around her, holding her close. 'Dex.'

'I've missed you, Iris.'

'Have you? Why?'

'I've missed talking to you. Spending time with you. Being with you.'

'Because of Anya?'

'No.' The word was wrenched from him. 'Not because of Anya. Because of *you*. You give me strength, Iris. You were there when I faced my family. You supported me through one of the most difficult times in my life and I was able to do it because of your inner strength. You urged me on. You made me believe in myself.' He reached around to the back of her hair and pulled the band from the back of her plait. 'I thought I was just some guy who would be wandering around in the desert for the rest of my life. I was unable to make a firm connection with anyone because I was so disconnected.' His fingers worked to free her hair and he touched the long tendrils delicately. Then he bent his head and pressed little kisses to the side of her cheek and around to her ear.

'You changed that, Iris. You talked to me, you opened me up simply by being yourself. You've been through so much and I admire you.'

Iris closed her eyes, trying to focus on the important words he was whispering to her as he pressed a blazing trail of kisses to her face. He worked his way down her neck and she tilted her head back to allow him access. She couldn't believe what he was saying. She'd helped him? Really helped him?

When he unbuttoned the top of her shirt, faint alarm bells started to ring but he kept kissing her, the heat of his lips on her skin almost like a drug, and it was a drug she craved. Another button was undone and the alarm bells started to ring even louder.

'Dex?' She whispered his name and put her fingers into his hair.

'Mmm. Your skin tastes like…'

'Like what?'

'Heaven.' He kissed her lower and her eyes flew open as his finger grazed over one of her scars.

'Dex!' She dug her fingers into his hair and wrenched his head back. Shock and total confusion were in his eyes. 'Don't. Don't touch me there.' She couldn't believe she'd been so stupid. Why had she let him go so far? Why hadn't she been able to resist him?

'You're angry?'

'I'm scarred, Dex.'

'I know, and I know why you're scarred, too. That makes no difference.'

'Oh, so what is this, then? Take pity on the woman who is so ugly no other man would ever want her? What am I to you? I told you I wasn't going to be another conquest.'

'What?' Dex couldn't believe what he was hearing. One second she was all relaxed and pliant in his arms and the next she was like a fire-breathing dragon. 'What? No. It's not like that at all.' He tried to gather her close again but she pushed him away. 'Iris.' He placed his hands on her shoulders and turned her to face him, her glorious mane of hair fanning out around her face, falling over his hands and down her back. 'Stop it. How could you even think that?'

'You're a playboy.'

'And you think that because in the past I've spent time in the company of other women, I'm taking pity on you?'

'The other women are beautiful. I know I'm not beautiful. It's a fact I'm reminded of every day.'

'You're insane, honey. How could you not think you're beautiful? Your eyes, which are flashing bright emerald fire right now, are so powerful I tremble with desire every time I look into them. And your hair.' He ran his fingers through her hair, the silky strands sparkling their glorious reddish-blonde. 'It's the most incredible colour and so long and luscious. I can't get enough of it and I get annoyed whenever you tie it back. And your skin. It's so soft, so special and so mind-numbing whenever you let me touch you. Iris. Of course you're beautiful. You're the most beautiful woman I've ever met.'

'No, I'm not.' She shook her head. His words, which she could hear filled with sincerity, were making her start to believe him. 'I'm strong.

I'm reliable. I helped you. You feel grateful. You're only—'

Dex cut her off by placing his lips angrily over her own. He pulled her to him and put everything into that kiss. Everything he was feeling. Everything he'd ever felt. Everything he'd hoped to feel. It was a whole second later that Iris kissed him back, matching his intensity as though she was punishing him for wanting her.

'I love you,' he ground out when he eventually let her up for air. 'I've been trying to fight it. Trying to figure things out. I was even considering leaving town just so you could stay here in Didja and raise Anya because it's the best place for both of you to be right now.'

'You were going to leave?' There was no anger in her words and although she wanted to believe him when he said he loved her, she still wasn't sure.

'I had to.' He looked away and then looked into her eyes again. 'When we got back from Perth, I realised how I felt about you. That's why I tried to put distance between us. With Anya in the picture, it only made matters worse. I don't think I'll make a very good husband and I don't think I'll make a very good father. I've made so many mistakes in my life, done so many stupid things that I couldn't bear it if I made a mistake and hurt you both. The only person who has ever really been there for me is Joss. And then Melissa came. And then…there was you. That's why it's so vitally important that I don't hurt you, that I don't screw up any more, and the only way I can do that is to let you go. You've been hurt too much in the past and I don't want to be responsible for inflicting more on you. I realised you've obviously seen these flaws in me because that's why you've been keeping your distance these past few weeks.'

Iris stared at him, her mind still trying to absorb the words he'd said. He loved her?

'You're insane,' she started, and then brought her lips to his, wanting him to feel how deeply wrong he was. She'd always thought there was no way he could possibly want her and now he was telling her that he loved her. He loved her so much he was willing to let her go? 'Don't you dare let me go,' she said, breathing heavily.

'What?' Dex shook his head. 'I'm dazed and confused.'

'You say you love me, right?'

'Yes. I'm sorry if that makes things more confusing for you but—'

She placed her finger across his lips. 'Shh. I need...I need to work this out.' She paused, trying to think logically, but it was so difficult when he was this close to her. 'You love me. Scars and all?'

'Emotional and physical scars.'

'You're not repulsed by them?'

'Repulsed? No. Iris, how could you think that?'

'Because I've been repulsed by them for so long.'

'They remind you of a bad time in your life but they're a part of you, a part of who you've become during these last four years. They symbolise your inner strength, your bravery.' He took her hands in his and looked into her gorgeous eyes. 'Will you show them to me?'

Iris wasn't at all sure at first but the more she thought about it, the more she realised that the sooner she got it over and done with, the sooner whatever illusions Dex was under about her being beautiful would disappear. He'd be as repulsed by them as she was. He'd let her go. He'd move on and she could get back to the life she was trying to carve out for herself with Anya. Alone.

'Please?' He looked at her with those brown puppydog eyes that were so difficult to resist, and without a word she started to unbutton her shirt.

Her fingers started to tremble after the first few buttons and Dex immediately helped her with the last few before the shirt hung limply open.

Her flesh-coloured bra was practical and sensible. The essence of Iris yet Dex knew it was just underwear and didn't really signify a thing. He brushed the shirt open a little further and then slipped it from her shoulders, marvelling at her natural beauty.

'Wow.' The word was a whisper.

'I know. Horrible, aren't they?'

'No. I meant *Wow*. You are… Lady, you're taking my breath away.'

'But…' Iris pointed to the scars on her abdomen, the ones higher up on her arms and then turned so she could show him the ones on her back, which had required skin grafts.

'Oh, honey.' There was pain in his voice now and a second later she realised he'd dropped to his knees and was brushing kisses across her scars. Iris gasped at the touch and closed her eyes. It was so intimate. So giving. So loving.

His hands were at her waist and slowly he turned her to face him before he proceeded to kiss the scars on her abdomen. Slowly, he kept kissing her, making his way up to the soft tissue around her cleavage. Then he nibbled her neck and then her ear and finally he placed a kiss on her lips.

'Beautiful. *All* of you.'

'I didn't think you wanted me. That's why I've been avoiding you.'

'You didn't think…' He stopped and shook his head. 'Iris, I've wanted you for far too long, my sweet, sweet lady. I've been crazy about you for ever. The life I was living before you arrived was more like an existence.'

He took a breath before continuing, knowing how important it was to get this moment right. If she turned him down… He couldn't think about it. 'Iris. If you'll let me… will you give me permission to… to court you? To date you. To spend time with you… and Anya, of course. I realise she's a big part of your life now but I want to take the opportunity to really get to know you, my lovely, beautiful Iris.'

'Oh, Dex. You really are insane. You love me? You want to date me? Court me?'

'I do. In the hope that one day, perhaps, you'll come to love me as much as I love you.'

Iris laughed. She couldn't help it but it was a laugh filled with utter joy and complete happiness. 'You won't have to wait long because that day is today.'

Dex looked at her, a puzzled frown on his brow. 'Today?'

'I love you, silly. I've loved you for weeks and it was only because I didn't think you wanted me that I…' She laughed again. 'Oh, we've both been such insane fools.'

Dex's gaze was one of complete truth. 'Insane fools in love.' He bent his head and brushed his lips across hers, and she sighed into his embrace. He wanted her. She wanted him. He loved her and she loved him. 'Can this be true?' he whispered against her mouth.

'Is this real?' she whispered back, before kissing him once more.

Anya, who was in the other room, gurgled loudly as though she was tired of being ignored by her two favourite people. Iris quickly pulled her shirt back on and followed Dex into the other room.

He scooped the baby up and kissed her cheek. 'I love her, Iris.'

'So do I.'

'She's going to need a mum and a dad around.'

'Agreed.' Iris tilted her head on the side. 'And I think I know the perfect person.'

'Ooh, pick me,' Dex said with a teasing grin.

'I do. What do you think, Anya? Shall we keep

him around?' The baby's answer was to snuggle into Dex and place her head on his shoulder. 'I'd take that as a yes.'

'I love you, Iris.' Dex pulled her close with his free arm and kissed her. 'I promise to do everything I can to make both you and Anya so very happy for the rest of my life. Please? Marry me?'

Iris smiled up at him, her heart happy and more content than it had ever been. A man who loved her, scars and all. A beautiful baby girl who brought her so much joy. 'You…both of you… make me so very happy. How could I not marry you, Dexter Crawford? You're the only man for me.'

Dex looked at Anya. 'What do you think? Was that a yes?'

Anya's answer was to smile and gurgle happily. Iris kissed the man of her dreams yet again.

'It's most definitely a yes.'

EPILOGUE

'AND now it is the time for the best man to do the toast speechy thing,' announced Stig, who was the master of ceremonies.

There was a round of applause and Dex stood up, swatting away flies. Even though the reception was being held in a marquee, it didn't stop the flies from getting in. He paused for a moment and looked around at all the people before them. His parents were there, and his siblings. Although it had been less than a month since he'd reconciled with them, all the anger and pain he'd felt at their betrayal had vanished.

'Thanks, Stig, and thanks for the mouth-watering food. It's delicious. Big clap for Stig, everyone.'

The room broke into applause yet again. When things quietened down, Dex turned to look at his sister.

'Melissa—the blushing bride. You look radiant. You came here to Didja on an insane mission of wanting to make contact with me, your biological brother. You were patient, you were kind and instead of paying all your attention to me, you fell in love with my best friend!' Everyone laughed at this. 'And it's just as well you did because I haven't seen Joss this happy in, like, for ever.'

Dex's smile was wide and bright, his heart filled with pride and brotherly love. 'You've given me so many great gifts, Lis. Not only do I have another sister but Joss is now officially my brother-in-law. That's awesome.'

More people laughed.

'But there's one other thing Lis has done and it's something for which I'll be for ever grateful.' Dex's gazed settled on Iris, dressed in a rich purple dress, her hair half swept back, the rest flowing loosely around her shoulders. His heart swelled with such powerful love that for a moment he lost all ability to speak.

'Lis was responsible for Iris coming to Didja.'

There were a few wolf-whistles coming from the crowd now but Dex ignored them. Iris was looking at him as though he'd hung the moon, and he wanted her to feel that way for the rest of their lives.

'Iris—the most stunningly beautiful maid of

honour in the world—has brought such love to my life. Along with Iris comes the gorgeous Anya.' He scanned the room for whoever was holding the baby now, so many people wanting to snuggle the child close.

'Over here,' Bub called.

'I should have known,' Dex remarked. 'I don't think any of us can get enough of that little girl. She's special to the whole town.'

'Hear, hear,' someone called, and at the round of applause that followed, Anya clapped her hands as well.

Dex held up his hands for silence and then raised his glass. 'I'd like to make three toasts and I don't care if it goes against any sort of etiquette because you'll probably have figured out by now that I'm not the etiquette type.'

'No kidding,' Bluey called, and people laughed again.

Dex waited for silence. 'Firstly—to family and friends.'

Dex directed his glass towards his parents and siblings. Everyone echoed the toast.

'Secondly—to the bride and groom.'

Everyone held their glasses in the direction of Melissa and Joss before echoing that toast.

He walked towards Iris and she stood, putting her arm around him as he held her close.

'Thirdly—to true love that lasts for ever.'

They clinked glasses and looked into each other's eyes.

'For ever,' Iris whispered and kissed him lovingly.

MEDICAL™

Large Print

Titles for the next six months...

September

THE DOCTOR'S LOST-AND-FOUND BRIDE	Kate Hardy
MIRACLE: MARRIAGE REUNITED	Anne Fraser
A MOTHER FOR MATILDA	Amy Andrews
THE BOSS AND NURSE ALBRIGHT	Lynne Marshall
NEW SURGEON AT ASHVALE A&E	Joanna Neil
DESERT KING, DOCTOR DADDY	Meredith Webber

October

THE NURSE'S BROODING BOSS	Laura Iding
EMERGENCY DOCTOR AND CINDERELLA	Melanie Milburne
CITY SURGEON, SMALL TOWN MIRACLE	Marion Lennox
BACHELOR DAD, GIRL NEXT DOOR	Sharon Archer
A BABY FOR THE FLYING DOCTOR	Lucy Clark
NURSE, NANNY...BRIDE!	Alison Roberts

November

THE SURGEON'S MIRACLE	Caroline Anderson
DR DI ANGELO'S BABY BOMBSHELL	Janice Lynn
NEWBORN NEEDS A DAD	Dianne Drake
HIS MOTHERLESS LITTLE TWINS	Dianne Drake
WEDDING BELLS FOR THE VILLAGE NURSE	Abigail Gordon
HER LONG-LOST HUSBAND	Josie Metcalfe

MILLS & BOON®